SUPERNOVA

L. B. GOLD

Chapter I
Oblivion

Teardrop after teardrop rained down from the Seattle sky. The gibbous moon had long since surrendered its celestial domain, its audacity cloaked by gunmetal clouds. Rapids raced atop the once orderly streets, raging against the very bedrock of civilization, reasserting the rule of nature over man. The savage waters vaulted the curbs and trespassed onto the vacant sidewalks, in blatant defiance of the cedar sentries who guarded them. Somewhere a power line must have been damaged, for nothing permeated the primordial black. Nearly every creature lay asleep, not daring to venture out into the apocalypse.

Seconds before midnight, a single star emerged between the clouds. Its faint glow delicately reflected off the inundated landscape, introducing if only for an instant a glimmer of brilliant light into the world. The star had in fact exploded a long time ago, but it would continue to shine for millennia. No one would know that it had died a spectacular death, that in a cataclysmic supernova it had been extinguished for all of eternity, that its light was merely a reminder of an ever-fading past. Then, without warning, that past was lost, the star slipped behind the clouds once more, and absolute darkness reigned supreme.

* * *

Arthur Noir clumsily grasped one of the dozen beers that stood half-empty on his kitchen counter. In a drunken stupor he dropped the bottle, only to be revived by the sound of shattering glass. Cursing incoherently, Arthur grabbed ahold of his flashlight and headed to the bedroom. In his nightstand drawer, he sifted through the artifacts of his criminality: several joints, a pistol, methamphetamine, and five stacks of twenty-dollar bills. Eventually locating his matches, Arthur lit a mostly melted candle, turned off the flashlight, and collapsed onto his bed. It had been a very long day indeed.

Arthur's gaze lazily meandered across his disheveled room, with the candlelight casting deathly shadows on his equally grim possessions. The alcohol he'd ingested earlier implored him to slumber, and he was about to do so when he became vaguely aware that something was out of place. In front of the doorway, he noticed a dark figure, a man perhaps. With mounting trepidation, Arthur strained to remember if he had let anyone into his house, but all he could think about was the wrathful pounding of the rain outside. Sweat began dripping from his forehead, while the blanket wrapped around him morphed into a Boa constrictor strangling his immobilized body.

Arthur glanced up again. Troublingly, the figure was still there. It was a man—he was certain of that now. And the man was holding something.

"Gun," said Arthur definitively, as if finally recalling the name of an old friend. He may have been drunk, but if there was one thing Arthur could recognize, it was a gun. The pieces slowly started coming together. The man was holding a gun. There was a man in his room, and he was holding a gun.

"Gun?" Arthur repeated, much less sure of himself this time. The booze was really starting to take effect now, and for a moment he lost interest in the whole gun business and closed his eyes. He would sleep off the beer and deal with everything in the morning, he decided. All the while, the man stood silently by the door, holding the gun, his glare fixed inexorably on Arthur.

*** * ***

Five minutes later, Arthur knelt before the man, fully awake now, begging for his life.

"Please don't kill me!" he cried. Arthur was hardly capable of eloquence given his present condition, and regardless this seemed like the wrong time for elevated discourse. "I haven't hurt anyone! I'm a good guy, I swear!" The man did not reply. In fact, he had yet to utter a single word, which was driving Arthur mad.

"Do you want drugs? Money? I have whatever you want!" The man said nothing. Instead, he stared at Arthur from the two tiny slits in his mask. His blue eyes were the only part of him not covered in black: two stars in the vastness of the universe, two glimmers of brilliant light from the depths of death personified. But those stars had already been extinguished, and that light was merely a reminder of an infinitely distant past.

"I'm a drug dealer," explained Arthur, almost proudly. "Look." He pointed to a score of plastic bags filled with fine powder. "I can make you rich. Please, man! Don't kill me! I'm a good guy!" Silence. Deathly silence. Suddenly, Arthur had a plan.

"Let me show you something," he said, pacing backward toward his nightstand. With a well-rehearsed air of indifference, he opened the drawer, while the man remained motionless. His pistol was right there; life was staring him dead in the face. Taking a deep breath and mustering all his courage, Arthur clasped the pistol and in one move brought it up across his body, aimed at the man, and pulled the trigger over and over again. The man still stood motionless, still decidedly alive.

A series of increasingly terrifying thoughts progressed through the consciousness of Arthur Noir at that moment. His pistol was empty. The man had emptied his pistol. He was going to die.

"Please," Arthur whispered, falling to the floor. "Please." The man looked into Arthur's eyes and saw his whole life: all his struggles and successes, his wishes and his fears. Teardrop after teardrop rained down from Arthur's soul.

The man fired the gun. The bullet went through Arthur's eye and into his brain, killing him instantly. The man pitilessly seized Arthur's legs and dragged his bleeding corpse through the house. He opened the front door, and both living and dead quickly became soaked. Without hesitation, the man shoved Arthur's body down the steps and into oblivion.

The sidewalk currents were quite fast by now, and the suburban swells carried Arthur to an unknown grave. His black blood mixed with the black river under the black sky, his death forgotten in a universe where life is the exception. The man removed his black gloves and his black mask. He threw his black jacket into the black house, and walked into the wet, black street. Nothing mattered now. It was over. It was finally over.

Chapter II
White

Anthony Wilson gazed with wonderment at the summer sky. The midday sun loomed especially large atop its kingdom, the shadows having succumbed to its shimmering glare. For what felt like an eternity, Anthony stared directly at the source of the light, making eye contact with the white sun. He was no longer subject to its panoptic supremacy, for at this moment, he was invincible.

Anthony felt a surge of pure energy overwhelm him. He began tearing up, with white streams of joy flowing down his cheeks and onto the pavement below. He glanced affectionately at his wife Isabelle, placing his hand upon her dress. The sunlight sparkled on her soft eyes, and she smiled back at him with pearly white teeth. In her arms she held something in a silk blanket, which she pressed firmly against her heart.

"Christopher," she whispered to the blanket.

"Christopher," Anthony echoed warmly. "You will always be loved."

Christopher looked up at the light of day for the first time, a picture of innocence and renewal.

Thousands of miles away, a flock of black crows soared toward young Christopher at breakneck speed. But in this moment, the world stood still, the sky was clear, and love cradled him in its white embrace. The crows would simply have to be patient.

* * *

Anthony was twenty-three years old when he discovered his raison d'être. After eight semesters of proving theorems in monochrome lecture halls, he was glad to be done with college and enjoying his summer abroad. He and a few friends were on vacation in the south of France, and on this particular afternoon they were exploring Aix-en-Provence.

Bored of the main road, Anthony wandered off alone. For an instant, he let himself be lost in the world, relishing the present rather than preparing for the future. Suddenly, everything was alive. The soulless automatons to his left materialized into a couple holding hands, while the sky radiated blueness of its own volition. Colors traded places impossibly between vibrant flower petals, cacophonous sounds somehow synthesized in perfect harmony. All around him wafted the mild aroma of freshly baked baguettes. Like never before, Anthony was overwhelmed by the profound immediacy of the moment at hand. If only he could remain so alive, so free, forever—liberated from the trappings of his own potential.

Amidst this infant paradise appeared a beautiful courtyard. Ornate little buildings flanked a garden of white daisies, while a small church with stained glass windows stood opposite him. A massive oak tree dominated the field, as it likely had since the beginning of time, beholding the world from its otherworldly post. Several children were playing in a marble fountain, their faces obscured by leaves twirling aimlessly in the warm breeze. Twilight illuminated the scene with a soft glow that enhanced its ethereal aura.

Safeguarded by the sacred tree and drinking from a cup of cheap champagne rested a fairy. Her light blonde hair flowed in waves onto her tiny shoulders, and her white shoes lay next to her delicate bare feet. She was easily the most amazing creature Anthony had ever seen. He approached cautiously, admiring her from the Edenic shade.

"Bonjour," he finally managed. "Je m'appelle Anthony." The fairy looked at him and smiled. Anthony smiled back, very pleased with himself. "Enchanté," he continued. And it was true. He was enchanted.

"Nice to meet you," replied the fairy in perfect English. "I'm Isabelle." Anthony laughed, somewhat embarrassed and entirely spellbound. Isabelle poured him a cup of champagne, and the pair sat in silence watching the leaves drift across the field. Then they kissed for a long time, needing no words or prior experiences to share in the intimacy of the moment. Until the birth of their son Christopher, that was the happiest day of their lives.

Anthony left his friends and stayed with Isabelle all summer long. Deeply in love, she agreed to move to Seattle—Anthony's hometown—where she passed the time writing flowery poems that went unread until the yellowed paper wilted. Anthony became a math teacher at a local high school, and together they struggled to carve out their own sliver of history.

Anthony of Washington and Isabelle of Provence were married the following summer, and only a year later Christopher was born. During that brief span, Anthony, who still viewed himself as an adventurous youth, had transformed into a responsible provider, a metamorphosis that had occurred without his knowledge inside a blinding chrysalis of passion. But now, sitting with his new family at his new table in his new home, Anthony was unconcerned with the past, for his life had only just begun.

Stacked on a desk behind him were the books that had once defined his existential worldview: *The Hitchhiker's Guide to the Galaxy*, *The Stranger*, and the somewhat more moralistic *Crime and Punishment*—which perhaps in recognition of its incongruity lay backward. As Anthony watched Christopher sleeping in his mother's arms, most of those works seemed highly inadequate, rendered obsolete by the sense of meaning Isabelle had bestowed upon him. Utterly content, he took a sip of cheap champagne and drifted into a state of pleasant nostalgia.

Chapter III
Jacket

Christopher carefully scrutinized his reflection, frowning with disapproval. His green shoes seemed to be fighting with his azure jeans for attention, while an asylum-wall-white polo shirt hung down close to his knees. Isabelle knelt beside her son, proudly assembling his increasingly ridiculous ensemble.

"Hold still," she insisted, spiking up the front of his freshly combed hair with thick gobs of white gel. She dipped her head for a moment and coughed several times, then turned back to complete her masterpiece. "Done. See, you look just adorable! Doesn't he look great, sweetheart?"

"Definitely," Anthony responded, before shooting Christopher a sympathetic smile. "Already a lady-killer."

"Just like his dad," Isabelle said.

"Do I really need to wear this shirt?" moaned Christopher.

Isabelle nodded. "You have to look handsome when you meet your classmates. First grade is a big deal." Christopher grudgingly accepted this reasoning and turned toward his father.

"Can we go now, Dad?"

"Are you sure you're fine with taking him?" asked Isabelle. "I'm not feeling that sick anymore."

"I'm happy to help," Anthony said. "It *is* an important day, after all." For a fleeting instant, Anthony saw himself from the outside—observed his physical form playing a role in the hackneyed drama that was his life. He had delivered his line, the words he was supposed to recite in this situation. Anthony felt flares of solar heat coursing through his veins and melting away his individuality, his very essence threatened by an invisible supernova. But he couldn't explode. There was simply too much to do.

"Let's go," said Christopher restlessly. Anthony snapped back into reality, engulfing Christopher's hand in his much larger fingers. The pair got into a dilapidated sedan and backed out of the driveway, the sputtering car still managing improbably to serve as a means of transport. Isabelle watched them depart in her white robe, smiling warmly before sneezing onto her toast.

As Anthony turned the corner, he glanced back at his son in the rearview mirror. Christopher was looking out the window with his ever-present grin, his hair protruding out wildly in random directions, having already escaped the gel's vain hold. That kid is going to be different, he thought. One day, he's going to be great.

"I was waiting until your mom couldn't see us anymore to give you this," Anthony said. He picked up a sleek black jacket from the passenger seat and handed it to Christopher. "Now you'll really be a stud."

"Thanks, Dad!" Christopher immediately put on the jacket and zipped it up to his neck, covering wimpy white with beastly black.

"Looks like no one will see that awful shirt your mother loves so much," Anthony said, as if talking to himself. Christopher giggled. His dad was so cool.

"Okay, buddy, we're here."

"Already?" asked Christopher, a wave of anxiety sweeping over him. He felt like cookie dough: about to be scorched and devoured just as his life was starting to take shape.

Anthony stopped the car and turned around. "How do you feel, Christopher?"

"Like cookie dough," he replied nervously.

His father laughed. "Is that a good thing?"

"No."

"Don't worry, Son. You're a genius. You'll be fine."

"Are you sure?"

"Absolutely. Just be yourself." Anthony smiled, admiring his credible portrayal of the encouraging father. Christopher on the other hand promptly decided it was bad advice and opened his door.

"Have a good day," said Anthony.

Christopher hopped out of the car and stared at the towering labyrinth that composed the elementary school. The other kids looked like giants; their backpacks alone were twice his size. Christopher whirled back around, but the car was gone. In a panic, he straightened the collar of his new black jacket, drawing upon its foreign powers. I can do this, he assured himself. I can do this.

"Good morning, lad. Are you lost?" Christopher turned around to find a portly Scotsman in a snowy woolen sweater.

"Yes, sir. My name is Christopher Wilson and I am in the first grade. Could you please show me where to go?

"Wow, you're quite a polite young man. Well, follow me. I'll walk you to your class." The man waddled through an ocean of students, with the trailing Christopher desperately trying to stay afloat. Only after multiple elbows and backpacks had bruised his face did he arrive in front of Room 42.

"Is this my class?" inquired Christopher. "Who's my teacher?"

"You'll find the answers to all your questions in there," said the man, pointing to the door. "I'm Principal Henderson, by the way."

"My dad told me not to see the principal," said Christopher innocently, closing his eyes. He really didn't want to make his parents upset on the very first day of school. Meanwhile, Principal Henderson laughed merrily and walked away.

"Bye," said Christopher, still with his eyes closed. Blindly, he headed in the general direction of the classroom. On his way there he bumped into a girl named Emily. She had dirty blonde hair and light brown eyes, with her red dress frilling ridiculously at the knees.

"Eww!" exclaimed Emily. "Cooties!"

"I apologize," said Christopher sincerely.

"You're weird."

"You're certainly entitled to your opinion," Christopher replied. His dad said that to his mom sometimes when she was angry.

"No, I'm not!" she countered defensively, quite confused. Christopher opened his eyes and smiled at Emily, a move she must not have anticipated because she sprinted off at full speed. Christopher watched her go. This was it. This was first grade.

Chapter IV
Dolls

Mrs. Wright inspected the new batch of students like a mechanic scanning for a defective part. There was always one troublemaker she would have to fix up by year's end, one young mind that required her experienced fine-tuning. For thirty-seven years, Mrs. Wright had made a living repairing those faulty faculties, ensuring that the educational assembly line operated at maximum efficiency.

Once upon a time, an innovative twentysomething strolled confidently into Room 42, imagining herself a maverick who would foster originality and shape the lives of her uniquely gifted pupils. But that naïve young woman quickly learned that creativity was dangerous and that conformity meant order. After nearly four decades of instructing student after student, she had come to understand that for every question there was a right answer and a wrong answer, in every instance there was a right way to act and a wrong way to act. For the sake of her own sanity, Mrs. Wright had long since decided that for all of those questions and in each of those instances, she would always be right.

"Hello, children," she said, with an affected warmth so subtly artificial that only Christopher felt uneasy. "Welcome to first grade. My name is Mrs. Wright, and I'll be your teacher this year."

Many of the students ignored the introduction and continued to play. A few whispered to each other and pointed toward Matthew, a red-haired boy in front of Mrs. Wright. Wholly absorbed in his personal universe, Matthew stood picking his nose with an air of supreme self-assuredness, pausing at regular intervals to appraise his findings.

"If you would all follow me into the classroom, we can get started." Mrs. Wright began walking to the door. "I am very excited to meet you all." She ascended the timeworn steps, ducked under the once white number 42, and entered her factory, with the new, bipedal raw materials in tow. While the other kids rushed inside, Christopher straggled behind. Standing atop the steps, he took one look back at the now empty schoolyard, paused reflectively, and then walked in to join his classmates.

* * *

Christopher paced through the passageways of the classroom, sweating from the heat of thirty pairs of eyes burning through his clothes. He was surrounded by perfect strangers: their backpacks below their desks, their white shirts and dresses draped over their torsos like parachutes, and their stares simmering on his smooth skin. On the surface, every child was quite different, but on some innate level they were all disconcertingly similar—plastic molded into identical dolls by an equally synthetic society.

In the farthest corner of the room, Christopher spotted the lone empty seat—a battered wooden object that had long ago given up masquerading as a chair. Worse still, it rested directly between Emily, who had apparently recovered from the cooties incident, and Matthew, who had finished excavating his nostrils and sat flicking himself on the forehead. *I really shouldn't have come inside last,* thought Christopher dejectedly, sporting a strained smile.

Meanwhile, Mrs. Wright, who had been watching him throughout, mistook his nervous grin for an arrogant smirk. In his dark jacket, Christopher was like a blotch of ink on a fresh sheet of paper. Mrs. Wright would thereupon make it her mission to white out that ink. She laughed reservedly: after a mere two minutes she had already isolated the defective part. Never in all her years as a teacher had Mrs. Wright failed to fix a glitch in her well-oiled machine, and this kid would be no exception. If only the world knew just how invaluable she was.

* * *

An hour later, the class sat listening to Mrs. Wright read from a standardized book with a glossy cover. Mrs. Wright herself had flipped through these pages at least fifty times by now, and this rendition was entirely automatic.

"The dog ran after the cat *very* fast," she recounted. "The cat was scared of the dog."

With her prefrontal cortex unoccupied, Mrs. Wright focused her concentration on the students. Each child stared back at her intently, looking at the colorful illustrations, their minds completely engaged by the plot of the story. And then she saw Christopher, resting his chin upon a closed fist like Rodin's *The Thinker*, his eyes glazed over, staring at the wall. Suddenly, Christopher looked up.

"Why was the dog chasing the cat?" he asked genuinely. Mrs. Wright hesitated for a moment.

"Because dogs chase cats," she responded after some deliberation. "That's just what they do."

"But why? That seems so mean. Unless..." Christopher slipped back into contemplation, and then looked up again. "Unless the dog wanted to *eat* the cat."

The other kids began chattering loudly, having never considered this possibility.

"That must be it," Christopher continued. "Dogs eat cats because they're carnivores."

This last revelation instigated a frenzy of dissonant shouting. Mrs. Wright stood up, having lost control of her own classroom. "Okay, everyone, settle down. I think it's about time we stop reading and practice our spelling."

Christopher was thoroughly disappointed, having just uncovered the dog's most consuming motivation. "Why?" he asked.

"That's a hard word," said Mrs. Wright. "Can anyone spell the word 'why'?"

Christopher sighed. Many of his classmates shouted out erroneous guesses, including "w-y," "u-y," and even "y" by itself. Christopher raised his hand.

"Yes, Christopher?"

"W-h-y," he said. "Now can we keep reading?"

Chapter V
Gold

Isabelle rested her head against the passenger side window, smiling broadly. Rain had doused Seattle all week long, but on this late autumn afternoon the sunshine had returned triumphant, a conquering hero flaunting the plundered promise of better days. Rejuvenating light radiated down with unseasonable intensity, vaporizing the last watery remnants of gloom. White, voluminous clouds wandered lazily across the sky, accentuating the ubiquitous calm.

Isabelle sighed contentedly—overcome with the heavenly feeling that everything was just as it was meant to be. It was a relatively new sensation, for her life hadn't always been so tranquil. Indeed, she had experienced many dreary days and nasty nights, but unfailingly, God had given her the strength to persevere. Only through him had she found virtue, had she discovered the polarized nature of right and wrong. Now, after all these years, she was able to share that knowledge with her progeny.

Far from a spiritual man himself, Anthony leaned back into the old, fabric driver's seat. He rested his left hand on the steering wheel, while with his right hand he held a rapidly collapsing cheeseburger. Yawning loudly, he turned toward Isabelle, who glowed both from the sun and from within. Though he cared little about religious fulfillment, he cared deeply about his wife, and seeing her present bliss made him regret his prior unwillingness to allow faith into their household. Christopher deserves to know what he's been missing out on, Anthony reasoned.

Christopher himself fidgeted excitedly in the backseat, donning an ill-fitting suit. His mother had told him many stories about Jesus and his powers, and although he personally preferred Superman, Jesus was still pretty awesome. Hopefully he would have a chance to meet him at church, or at the very least learn more about him.

An amber leaf landed delicately on the windshield, then drifted off the car as Anthony turned into the parking lot. He looked back at Christopher and smiled. This is going to be fine, he assured himself.

Anthony pulled into one of the last vacant spots, Isabelle lifted her head as if awakening from an interminable dream, and Christopher flung his door open with long-accumulated energy. Man and wife stayed put, savoring the idyllic serenity of their temporary sanctum. They stared into each other's eyes with a togetherness that was more peaceful than romantic. No words were said; no words were needed.

"Let's go!" Christopher yelled, banging on the door. Anthony and Isabelle crawled out of the car, and the Wilsons began walking toward a grand cathedral.

The walls were adorned with shimmering stained glass, highlighted by a brilliant rose window on the western façade that glistened in the sunlight. Christopher ran ahead of his parents and approached the entrance in awe. He felt as though he were standing at the very center of the universe, with everything else in existence merely serving as a backdrop for this supreme site. God must have been very pleased with the extravagance of his golden shrine.

"Christopher!" Isabelle called out. "Hold on for a second."

"What is it, Mom?" he replied.

"I have something for you." She reached into her purse and removed a small, white box. "It's sort of a family heirloom."

"What's an heirloom?"

"It's a special thing that gets passed down in a family, like a tradition. I got it from my mother, she got it from her father, and now I'm giving it to you."

"You're giving me a box?" Christopher asked. Anthony, who had anticipated this misunderstanding, laughed heartily and patted Christopher on the head.

"No, sweetie. I'm giving you this." She opened the box to reveal a gold cross necklace. "This is very precious to me, which is why I want you to have it." She looped the thin chain over Christopher's neck, with the cross itself hanging down to his stomach. Isabelle looked at Christopher and smiled proudly.

"What is it?" asked Christopher.

"It's a symbol of Jesus. It represents God's love for you and all his children. It's called a cross."

Christopher's face lit up. Superman had an "S" on his chest, so logically Jesus ought to have a logo as well.

"Does this mean that I'll have Jesus's powers too?"

Isabelle thought for a moment. "Well, yes, actually. You will always have Jesus's courage to give you strength."

This seemed like a good deal to Christopher, who gave his mother a tight hug. Anthony watched the scene unfold in silence, becoming progressively edgier beneath his fixed grin.

"Look up there, Christopher," said Isabelle, pointing to the top of the steeple in front of them. "Can you see what that is?"

"A cross?"

"A really big cross. Just like the one you're wearing."

Christopher was beyond elated with his present. Suddenly he had a distressing thought.

"What happens when I take the necklace off?" he asked with concern. "Will I still have Jesus's courage?"

"Jesus will be with you no matter what," Isabelle assured him. "Do you know why I named you Christopher?"

"No."

"Your name means 'bearing Christ.' Jesus will always stay with you, even when you're not wearing the cross.

"What does your name mean, Mom?"

"Isabelle means 'devoted to God.' Names help to show us who we are."

25

"I think it's time to go inside," Anthony said disruptively. Isabelle turned toward her husband and kissed him tenderly on the cheek.

"Your dad's right," she said. "Let's go." With Christopher leading the way, the trio passed under the elaborate doorway and settled on an empty oaken pew near the back. Christopher sat in the middle, between his pious mother and his secular father, at the crossroads of faith and reason. After some time a bell resounded through the chamber, and the congregation rose in unison.

"Here we go," whispered Christopher, brimming with enthusiasm. Anthony squirmed uncomfortably. Here we go, he mentally echoed.

Chapter VI
Providence

Thunder boomed down from the heavens as Father Goodson finished his sermon. "May God bless you all," he concluded, his voice barely audible over the roar of raindrops hammering the ancient roof. The weather had taken a sudden and sinister turn as day gave way to night, with the lazy afternoon clouds revealing their stormy intentions. The stained glass windows, which had shone magnificently just hours ago, were now only illuminated for milliseconds at a time when lightning flashed nearby. The entire building, normally a bastion of hope and optimism, had transformed into a safe haven for doom.

The Wilsons exited the church and took cover under Anthony's sizable overcoat. Christopher looked back at the cathedral. A prodigious flock of crows idled along the buttresses, basking in the menacing atmosphere. At least a couple thousand of them uniformly lined the walls, though it was impossible to determine exactly how many there were amidst the darkness. Every bolt of lightning revealed dozens more flying onto the house of worship and settling on an empty spot. It was an utterly terrifying spectacle, made all the more frightening by the fact that the crows appeared to be staring directly at Christopher.

The crow is quietly one of nature's most fascinating creatures. Despite its diminutive size, it is remarkably intelligent, with brainpower approaching that of apes and monkeys. Astoundingly, crows have the ability to remember individual human beings, even squawking when they recognize ones that they dislike. Crows have historically been regarded as a symbol of death; in fact, the official name for a flock of crows is a murder. Perhaps over time the crow became too clever to be satisfied with its monotonous existence and inevitably identified with life's end, too analytical to don the naïve white color of the dove and opted instead for disillusioned black.

A preposterously thick lightning bolt suddenly struck the cross atop the steeple. The metal lit up the sky with an otherworldly shade of blue, while the sound of thunder reverberated with unearthly power. The crows scattered composedly off into the night, not out of fear but rather finality. Christopher jumped into the car, deeply shaken. The crows had certainly made their point.

"You all right, buddy?" Anthony asked, throwing his soaked overcoat next to Christopher.

"I'm fine," he replied unconvincingly. "Can we go home, please?"

"Of course." Anthony pulled out of the spot and merged onto the street, waves of water splashing violently onto the windows with every turn.

"So, what did you think?" asked Isabelle.

"He wasn't there," said Christopher, shaking from the cold.

"Who wasn't there?"

"Jesus."

Isabelle laughed. "I suppose not. What about the service, though? Did you like listening to Father Goodson?"

"It was okay," said Christopher. "How does he know so many stories? Is he really old?"

"No, sweetie. He was talking about things that are written in the Bible."

"What's the Bible?"

"The Bible is a very important book that God wrote a long time ago. It tells us how to behave, how the world began, and what happens when we die."

Christopher thought about this for a moment. "How do you know God wrote the Bible?" he wondered aloud.

"Because my parents told me so," she said.

"But how did they know?"

"I guess their parents told them."

Christopher seemed troubled by this explanation. "But what if someone just made it all up?"

"Christopher..." Anthony warned.

"No, it's fine," said Isabelle. "You just need to have faith."

"What's that?" Christopher asked.

"Faith means knowing in your heart that something is true."

Christopher thoroughly searched his being, and then said, "I don't think I have faith."

"Sure you do," said Isabelle. "I have faith."

"Do you have faith, Dad?" Christopher asked sincerely.

"Christopher..." Isabelle cautioned.

"It's all right," Anthony said. "No, Son. I don't have faith."

Isabelle took a long glance at Anthony, who stared fixedly at the road ahead. Rain began pouring down harder than seemed possible, with the windshield wipers struggling to keep pace.

"Dad, do you think God is real?" asked Christopher.

"Of course he does," Isabelle said abruptly.

"Dad?" persisted Christopher. Isabelle's eyes locked in on Anthony's nervous face. There was a lengthy pause.

"No," he said finally. "No, I don't."

"Anthony!" exclaimed Isabelle, shocked.

"Well, he asked the question and—"

"It doesn't matter!" she shouted.

"I was just being honest with him." Anthony turned around to look at his son. "Hey, Christopher. Just because—"

Out of the corner of his eye, Anthony caught a glimpse of a black truck rapidly skidding toward the intersection, completely out of control. But it was too late: the pickup slammed senselessly into the right side of the car, sending a wall of rainwater towering into the night sky. Isabelle was immediately knocked unconscious, while Anthony's forehead hit the steering wheel before his airbag could go off. Christopher's skull smashed into the door on the far side of the backseat, opening up a large gash across his face and causing him to pass out as well. Glass from the two right windows shattered and flew into the car, digging into Christopher's skin. Lacerations leaked onto the fabric seats; bruises blackened in the undue destruction. After two seconds normalcy was restored, and everything fell silent.

Chapter VII
Promise

Christopher awoke into a white abyss. He blinked repeatedly, squinting as his vision became incrementally less blurry. Bullets of pain shot through his head, air drifted over the cracked desert soil that lined his throat, and his entire body throbbed rhythmically with his heartbeat. He had the vague sensation of being simultaneously burned alive and frozen solid, which was less than pleasant. His mother had once told him about hell, and now he was most definitely there.

Across the room, Christopher eventually discerned a row of cartoon faces displayed on a shiny poster, which was somewhat contemptuously titled "How Do You Feel?" The leftmost face was grinning above the injurious caption "No Pain," while the one on the opposite end was crying hysterically, with the phrase "Hurts Worst" penned below it. Christopher wasn't sure if he was crying. He couldn't feel his face.

"Mom," he screeched aridly. He looked around, his neck protesting every movement with sharp flares of anguish. He tried to get up, but to no avail. Indeed, he could barely feel his legs. Suddenly, Christopher was terrified. "Mom!" he screamed.

Anthony, who had fallen asleep in a chair beside his son, slowly opened his eyes. "Christopher?" he called out. "Christopher?"

"Dad?"

"Christopher!" Anthony disregarded his numerous leg contusions, deliriously springing to his feet and hugging the boy, who still lay motionless.

"What time is it?" asked Christopher blearily. Anthony took a second to put those words together, and then checked his watch.

"Five o'clock," he said.

"In the morning?"

"I don't know," Anthony replied honestly. Just then a man rushed into the room.

"He's back, Dr. Peterson!" Anthony cried ecstatically.

Dr. Peterson smiled with relief. He had heard screaming and feared the worst.

"He's talking and everything," Anthony continued. "Christopher, can you feel this?" Anthony flicked him on the knee.

"Ow," groaned Christopher. Dr. Peterson looked at Anthony warmly.

"Thank God," he said. "Thank God."

* * *

Christopher planted both of his feet on the hospital floor. With his body still resting on the bed, he gradually shifted his weight from his back to his legs. Every tiny twitch of a muscle revealed a new ache or bruise. It had been more than two weeks since the accident, and he had yet to take a single step.

"C'mon, buddy," Anthony encouraged. "You can do it." Christopher rose from his cot with brutal slowness, until finally he stood upright facing Dr. Peterson.

"Ugh," he complained.

"You're doing great, Christopher," said Dr. Peterson. "Now, walk over here." Christopher slid his right foot forward, then his left. His confidence building, he lifted his foot off the ground, collapsing immediately.

"Christopher!" exclaimed Anthony.

"It's fine," said Dr. Peterson. "Get up, Christopher. I believe in you." Christopher resolutely lifted himself up, his eyes revealing a determination not common in a boy of six. He took baby step after baby step, until after some time he reached the doctor.

"Well done," said Dr. Peterson, picking Christopher up and laying him back on the bed. "We'll do this again tomorrow. For now, get some rest." He walked out of the room and closed the door.

Christopher sighed. Resting is all he had done for the past half-month. He wasn't sure which form of torture he despised most: the agony of trying to move or the frustration of keeping still.

"I'll be back, Son," Anthony said. "Great job today."

"When is Mom going to come visit me?" Christopher asked.

"Soon, buddy. Really soon."

"Promise?"

Anthony hesitated. "Promise," he vowed, opening the door. "I love you, Christopher."

"Bye, Dad." Christopher watched his father leave the room. The lights beamed down with excruciating luminance, but he lacked the energy to turn them off. He pulled a thin blanket past his shoulders and closed his eyes, not because he was tired but because there wasn't much else to do. After ninety minutes, Christopher finally fell asleep, dreaming about his mother.

Chapter VIII
Elemental

Humans are to stars as a boy is to his mother. The elements that compose skin and bones and DNA—the very essence of human life—once fused together within a dying star, just as the boy formed inside his mother's womb. The sun emanates heat and vitality, while the mother gives her son warmth and love. There are many stars in the universe; there are many mothers in the world. But only one, chosen not by merit but by circumstance, is indispensable. When that one is gone, it is gone forever. When it dies, all that made sense falls apart, all that was light becomes dark. And despite its bygone resplendence, its supernova leaves only blackness in its stead.

Forty-two days after the accident, Isabelle Blanche Wilson passed away. Her brain damage had long ago rendered her comatose, but only after weeks of extensive testing and treatment did the doctors determine that she was, as they put it, no longer viable. Ultimately, the decision to cut off her life support had rested on Anthony. That dreadful evening, as his wife's hand grew cold against his own, he had felt something comparable to envy. Isabelle, sprawled emotionlessly on the white sheets, still looked livelier than he did, as his was undoubtedly the greater pain.

More than anything else, Anthony was angry. Of all people, why her? Why Isabelle? She had never thought of herself, only of others. She had never taken, only given. Clearly, thought Anthony, there is no God, for God would never kill an angel. All the while, Isabelle's last words echoed over and over in his head, like the tintinnabulation of a church bell. "It doesn't matter!" tolled the voice. "It doesn't matter!"

"Sir," someone called out. "We're ready to begin."

"Oh, Father Goodson," Anthony replied faintly. "I just need another minute."

Father Goodson looked at his watch impatiently. "It would be best if we started now."

"All right, then," said Anthony. He followed the priest outside into the December cold.

"You might want to get your coat."

"I'm fine," Anthony intoned. He didn't need a coat: he was completely numb.

"Would you like to speak at the beginning or at the end?"

"I don't know."

"At the end, then. That will give you some time to sort out your feelings."

"I have too many feelings to sort," said Anthony matter-of-factly. The pair continued walking into the fog, their destination hidden behind the white winter mist.

"Your wife is being buried close to the church," said Father Goodson with a vacuous smile. "That's a very good thing."

"A very good thing," Anthony repeated mindlessly. Isabelle's voice was getting louder and louder. "It doesn't matter!" she called from the grave. "It doesn't matter!"

* * *

Not more than twenty people surrounded the casket. They were Anthony's family and coworkers, Isabelle's former friends, and Principal Henderson, who looked unusually morose. Isabelle had not been particularly close with her family, who were nevertheless too poor to even consider flying to Seattle for her funeral. Christopher stood next to his father, wearing the same suit he had worn to church on that fateful day. Indeed, it was his only suit, though Anthony had given him a black tie for solemnity. With this new addition, somehow the entire outfit seemed to fit better.

Christopher watched his mother get lowered into the ground, not fully grasping the severity of the events unfolding before him. No one was crying—not even his father—so he abstained as well. But he was sad. Very, very sad. He knew his mom got to go to heaven and meet Jesus, so that was good. But he missed her a lot, and spent most of his time thinking about her. He either denied or didn't understand that she was gone forever; all that mattered was that she wasn't here in the present. She wasn't here to stand next to him and tell him that everything was going to be fine. She wasn't here to tell him that she loved him.

Christopher pulled the cross on his necklace up to his face and gazed into its metal heart. Recently, he had been unable to visualize his mother, and he certainly didn't want to see any pictures of her. But now, she appeared as if by magic, beaming back at him from the golden portal in his hand. He suddenly remembered sitting on her lap, stroking her hair while listening to her read a story. He must have only been three or four years old, and everything in the memory was blurry save for her kind eyes looking lovingly into his. Christopher realized at that moment that he would never see those eyes again. A single tear ran down his cheek and fell onto the grass below.

"Goodbye, Mom," he said quietly.

* * *

Long after the ceremony had concluded, Anthony returned to Isabelle's grave, finally alone with his everlasting love. Even in death, he would never leave her. Principal Henderson had offered to take Christopher bowling, a proposition to which Anthony had readily consented. It had been extremely difficult maintaining his poise for the boy, putting on his paternal mask when underneath he was utterly lost. Now, with Christopher gone, he was free to delve into the darkest depths of his desires. How he wished to be buried alongside his wife, to dissipate with her into their own private nothingness. Ultimately, though, he knew he couldn't join her there, nor could he take off his mask. There was still too much to do.

Anthony stared at the tombstone for what seemed like eons. "Bonjour," he said at last, introducing himself to the inanimate rock. "Je m'appelle Anthony." Man and wife sat together, needing no words or tangible connection to share in the intimacy of the moment. Then Anthony cried for a long time, his numbness slowly wearing off. The setting sun lit up the winter sky with a surreal shade of red, while a calm wind swept in from the west. Anthony felt the breeze blow away his tears as he basked in the love of days gone by.

Chapter IX
Plasma

Christopher meandered along a paved walkway toward distant railroad tracks, not entirely sure of his intentions. "Platform 10" read the sign atop a nearby stone column. That didn't seem right, so Christopher continued on. All around him, peddlers of every conceivable shape screamed their sales pitches discordantly, competing against each other for attention. They were wasting their time: Christopher was the only one there and he didn't have a wallet, much less any money. Ignoring the chaos, he focused instead on the "Platform 9" placard ahead of him.

Christopher started panting—the tracks seemed to be getting farther away with each step he took forward. Meanwhile, the salesmen multiplied at an alarming rate; soon there were hundreds, maybe thousands. Worse, they began to encircle Christopher, forming a whirlpool of gesticulating hands and assorted merchandise. The vortex of vendors violently swirled inward, compelling him to walk faster and faster toward the "Platform 8" marker. The sound of the salesmen was deafening—their collective roar stifled all sensible thought, while their voices remained indistinguishable.

One of the more importunate peddlers reached out and grabbed his arm, yelling incoherently in his direction. Squirming free in terror, Christopher bolted toward the pillar labeled "Platform 7," which as he zipped by it melted inexplicably and drained into a sea of lava. "Platform 6" was behind him in an instant. "Platform 5." The salesmen were becoming increasingly aggressive, and soon Christopher found himself sprinting with both arms extended, knocking the ones in front of him to the ground. Strangely, they fell like dominoes, their bodies putting up no resistance against his manic charge. But there were so many of them. Infinitely many.

The tracks were getting close by now, and Christopher could just hear the train thundering along in the distance. He looked up. Where the ceiling should have been, he saw the sky. It was flashing orange and purple in alternating streaks, which intersected perpendicular lines of black crows to form a disorienting checkerboard pattern. "Platform 4."

Christopher was moving as quickly as was physically possible—quicker, in fact. His surroundings became a uniform haze as he surpassed the speed of light, with the notable exception of the salesmen clinging to his consciousness. At the same time, his gold cross pounded against his chest, until eventually it knifed through his skin and stabbed his beating heart.

Christopher shot past a column with only the number "3" scribbled onto it by hand. As he did so, everything went quiet except for a couple of the vendors, whose booming voices bounced across the walls of the roofless station. One of them was Mrs. Wright, holding her glossy book with a frown, screaming "silence" over and over again. Another was Father Goodson, brandishing a leather-bound Bible whilst hawking his spiritual wares. Sweat poured down Christopher's back and into a small stream forming behind him. "2."

He was almost at the tracks now, with the train rolling in ever so slowly. The door to the foremost railcar was wide open, and inside it stood Isabelle, beckoning to him with ghostly waves. Christopher had overtaken the salesmen, and the path to his mother was clear. Then, out of nowhere, the final vendor appeared. It was a man, wearing a giant cross and a silken robe, repeating the word "faith" in a hypnotic and unsettling fashion. Somehow he knew the man was Jesus.

Christopher tried to slow down, but he was paralyzed. Suddenly, his rocketing body was strapped to a hospital bed, leaving him unable to stop his momentum or lower his arms.

"No!" Isabelle shouted. But it was too late. Christopher slammed into Jesus, who vaporized instantaneously. "1."

Christopher, now unfettered, continued forward and jumped onto the train. He reached for his mother, but she was already gone, never to return. He saw her running on the opposite side of the walkway, distancing herself from him and his reality.

"Mom!" Christopher cried inaudibly. She passed the final column. "0." The whole building ionized into plasma—starlike—before everything, even the once radiant Isabelle, went black.

* * *

Christopher flung himself out of bed, completely drenched in sweat. He must have called out in his sleep, because just then his father raced into his room.

"Is everything all right, Christopher?"

"What? Where? Dad?"

"You must've had a nightmare, buddy," said Anthony, relieved. He hugged Christopher, who was shaking with unshakable fear. "It's okay, Son. I'm here. I've got you." Anthony tightened his hold. "I've got you."

"I dreamed about Mom," said Christopher tearfully.

"So did I," admitted Anthony.

"I feel lonely."

"I know, Christopher. But remember, I'm still here, and I'll always be around when you need me. That much I can promise."

The two of them sat there the rest of the night, reminiscing about Isabelle, with only the other's company keeping them sane. In the morning Anthony made toast, which he burned. He was going to have to learn a lot of new things. Christopher went to school for the first time in nearly two months, and on the surface, everything was back to normal. But fundamentally, nothing was real. Nothing mattered. Anthony and

Christopher kept going solely out of routine; the train that was their lives quietly rolled onward into the unknown.

Chapter X
Gray

Christopher peered out the backseat window of the muted beige rental, a man in boy's clothes. Along the left side of his face ran a crimson scar, still bright from the accident. His black hair, formerly long and wild, was cut short and combed conservatively off to the side, while his once vibrant, baby-blue eyes were now indigo lochs undisturbed by human life. A slate-colored shirt extended past his waist onto a pair of ashen jeans, and his gold cross lay hidden under his black jacket.

Anthony saw his son in the rearview mirror, or at least what was left of him. The innocent little boy he had driven on that first day of school was gone, replaced by this gray, inconspicuous wraith. Anthony looked at his hands on the steering wheel. They looked gray as well, with new wrinkles running across them endwise to match his wizened complexion.

Glancing to his right, Anthony remembered stashing Christopher's jacket on the passenger seat all those weeks ago, all those centuries past. The calendar claimed he was thirty-one, but his brain knew better. Inside, he was ancient. He had experienced so much, loved so passionately, and lived so thoroughly that much of him was no longer alive at all.

Anthony pulled up to the curb. "We're here, buddy," he said. "Are you ready?" Christopher nodded and grabbed his backpack. "Have a good day, Son."

Christopher closed the door and Anthony drove away. He turned onto a tree-lined road, taking his foot off the accelerator, allowing the car to drift forward. The leaves had just started to come back; Spring was slowly usurping Winter's throne. But old king Winter was still sovereign over the land—the leaves only masked the barren emptiness that refused to fade away. Anthony was powerless to escape his misery. There was nothing to do. There was nowhere to go. Despite the revitalizing promise of Spring, Anthony remained subject to Winter's harsh reign.

Rain began falling softly on the car, dropping noiselessly onto the windshield. Not quite noiselessly— indistinctly perhaps. Muted. The trees blurred in the gray fog. Anthony pulled over, unable to continue. Don't do this, he told himself. He had a job, a child to feed. There was no time for this. But ultimately he struggled in vain: a pervasive melancholy infiltrated his mind and held him hostage. So Anthony sat in his car, in the rain, in silence. He was going to be late.

* * *

Christopher hurried inside Room 42 as the rain began to fall. He took his seat between Matthew, who stared at him blankly, and Emily, who was quiet. The rest of the class watched him with ill-concealed fascination. He had been gone for some time, though few of his classmates knew why.

Mrs. Wright approached Christopher and patted him on the shoulder. "Welcome back," she said warmly. "I'm glad you're here."

"Thanks," he responded.

"Are you ready to learn?"

"Probably," he said. Mrs. Wright smiled and then walked back to her desk.

Christopher turned toward Matthew, who had begun weaving his fingers together into a convoluted knot. He was totally fixated on the mechanics of it, oblivious to the outside world. Christopher wished he were like Matthew: able to lose himself in simple tasks rather than constantly thinking about the meaning of things.

Christopher spun around. Emily looked back at him unflinchingly, with profound understanding.

"I heard what happened to your mom," she said. "I feel bad for you."

"Thanks," said Christopher.

"Are you okay?" she asked compassionately.

"I think so."

"What's that?" Emily pointed at Christopher's scar.

"I cut my face in the accident."

"At least you didn't die," she said bluntly.

"All right, class, it's time to get started," announced Mrs. Wright. "Who can tell me the solution to ten minus three?"

Christopher raised his hand.

"Yes, Christopher," she said, happy that he was already participating.

"Seven," he stated confidently.

"Very good, Christopher," said Mrs. Wright. I guess he's not going to have trouble catching up, she thought.

"Just like how one hundred minus thirty is seventy," Christopher blurted out against his will. "And one thousand minus three hundred is seven hundred."

Mrs. Wright paused, clearly surprised. "Exactly," she said. "Okay, let's try another one. Does anyone know what eleven plus nine equals?"

Christopher's hand shot up again.

"Someone besides Christopher," she said. Emily raised her hand.

"Emily."

"Twenty?" she guessed.

"Well done," cooed Mrs. Wright. "We have a smart table back there."

Emily looked at Christopher and smiled. He smiled back. Matthew smiled too: his hands looked funny.

* * *

Christopher was deep in thought during the drive home from school. The day had not been nearly as bad as he thought it would be—actually, it had gone fairly well. He had answered all the questions right, for once. Mrs. Wright always corrected him when he tried to say something interesting, so he had forced his brain to turn off and only say the boring answers.

Even better, Christopher had made his first friend, Emily, who vaguely reminded him of his mother. Something about her was almost magical, but he wasn't sure exactly what. All he knew was that he liked being with her, and he wanted to be with her more. Christopher's classmates were constantly telling him that he was weird, so today he had been careful to act exactly like everyone else, and sure enough the day had passed without incident. Just then, Christopher had his first grand epiphany: if he blended in, his life would be much simpler. It was hard to stand out, to be white or black. But it was easy to be gray.

Mrs. Wright sat alone at her desk, mentally replaying the day's events. She had fixed the glitch in her assembly line much earlier than she had anticipated. Indeed, Christopher had every reason to be especially rebellious given his circumstances, but to her delight he had been exceptionally well mannered. She had known immediately how bright he was, how much potential he had. And now that she had fixed him up and given him some fine-tuning, he was ready to capitalize on that potential. From now on, Mrs. Wright thought gleefully, Christopher will be all right.

* * *

Anthony and Christopher sat at the table, eating Chinese food in silence, trying not to look at the empty chair.

"I made a friend today," said Christopher suddenly.

"Really, buddy?

"Yeah. Her name's Emily."

"Wow, that's fantastic."

"I tried acting like everybody else, and it worked."

Anthony leaned back into his chair, frowning. "Come with me, Christopher." Anthony got up and Christopher followed him onto the porch. The clouds had run out of rain and disappeared, leaving the night sky spectacularly clear. Father and son sat together on a wooden bench, looking up at the myriad stars.

"What do you want to be when you grow up?" asked Anthony.

"I don't know," Christopher replied.

"Do you have any ideas? You could be a scientist or a doctor or an astronaut..."

"I guess I want to be like you, Dad."

Anthony sighed. "Don't do that," he said.

"Why not?"

"When I was your age, I was a lot like you. I was smart—not as smart as you are—but smart nonetheless. I was curious. I was creative. My teachers told me that I would be president someday."

"You can still be president," said Christopher seriously.

Anthony laughed. "I could have been, maybe. But one day I decided that I didn't want to be different; I didn't want to stand out from the crowd. So I blended in, never saying what I really thought, never challenging myself. At first it was hard, but it got easier and easier until I forgot who I really was. And I didn't remember that until..." Anthony paused. "Until your mother died."

"Who are you?" asked Christopher, confused.

"I'm not like them, that much I know. You are certainly not like them. You're different. Look, I understand wanting to fit in and make friends—I get it. But that leads you down a path. It's the path that I followed. Sure, there are nice things on the path: you get good grades, you go to college, you get a job, you find love, you have kids. But that's all there is. There's no mystery or adventure or choice. And once you're on the path, there's no turning back. You get stuck. I'm stuck."

"You're stuck?" asked Christopher with concern.

"I'm fine. I have you, and I love you. I love you so much. But trust me, you're destined for more. Don't follow the path." Anthony pointed at a particularly bright dot in the sky.

"That's you," he said. "You are a star. You are brilliant. You are powerful. You are going to change the world. I don't know how. I don't know when. But you will, Christopher. You are a star."

Chapter XI
Suited

The Wilsons' financial situation had significantly improved in the four and a half years since Isabelle's passing. Anthony had been promoted three times, rising from the serfdom of the classroom to the comparative royalty of the principal's office. He had initially taken the job as a remedial math teacher with the principalship as his ultimate goal, and yet only after his wife's death and the resulting loss of his professional ambition did his meteoric rise begin. Congratulatory family and friends attributed his rapid ascension to his intelligence, while envious fellow teachers cited pity as the primary factor. Anthony himself cared little why he was placed in charge of North Valley High School. His sole concern was his son's happiness, and to that end, this new post was quite useful.

On this particular afternoon, the last day of school, Anthony was on high alert. While the students rejoiced in their newfound freedom, he struggled to thwart the inevitable pranks and shenanigans of the recently graduated seniors. Were it not for his efforts, toilet paper, graffiti, and the occasional outlandishly festooned teacher's car would decorate the campus by day's end. Personally, he found these minor acts of rebellion quite amusing. Professionally, he would not tolerate such blatant disregard for school policy.

An inhuman roar reverberated through the halls as the bell sounded for the final time. Anthony breathed a sigh of relief: notwithstanding the obligatory mural of obscenities sprayed onto his door, he had escaped the day practically unscathed. He began to collect his belongings, reflecting on the bizarre turn of events that had ultimately led him to this moment. He looked at his desk, where "Principal Wilson" was engraved into a gold-finished nameplate. Cynicism had long belittled his every achievement, and so—weary of reason—he had resolved to take pride in this shiny veneer of importance.

How far he had come in so little time, how profoundly different his life was now. It had been a year to remember, for sure—a great year, in fact. Anthony thought about this concept: had he really been, dare he say it, *happy*? Christopher was doing well in school, they had enough money, and people respected him. Why shouldn't he be content, at the very least? It seemed ungrateful not to be.

Anthony was about to leave the office when the phone rang. He grudgingly dropped his stuff and picked it up.

"Hello?" he said. Silence. "Hello?"

"Who is zis?"

"Anthony Wilson," he replied. "May I ask who's speaking?"

"I am Jean Dubois with zee government of France. I am calling to tell you zat your sister-in-law has passed away. I am very sorry."

"I think you have the wrong person," said Anthony perplexedly.

"No, it says right here…Blanche, Alice. Sibling of Blanche, Isabelle."

Anthony thought back. He vaguely recalled Isabelle mentioning an estranged sister. If he remembered correctly, it was something about drugs. That's probably how she died, he inferred.

"Sorry," said Anthony. "My wife and her sister were not close. Did she have any children?"

"Actually, sir, zat is zee reason for zis call."

* * *

Christopher, now eleven years of age, looked out the ovoid window as the plane took off. In many respects, he had completely transformed. His attitude and attire had both lightened substantially, and his glowing smile had returned. But beyond the superficial, he was still the same boy; he still carried with him a darkness that shaded his resplendence and cast shadows on his reality.

Christopher felt his surroundings begin to tilt skyward. He had never flown before—they had never had the money before—and this experience was thus both exhilarating and terrifying. He gripped the armrest tightly and pressed his body against his chair, as if bracing himself for the big drop on a roller coaster. He turned toward his father, who smiled back at him.

"Pretty cool, right?" he said.

"Crazy!" responded Christopher earnestly. He spun back toward the window. The airport was getting smaller and smaller as the airplane climbed higher and higher. Soon the cars became ants, and the people vanished entirely. After about a minute, he could see all of Seattle, his whole world reduced to a single point beyond the glass.

At that moment, Christopher had his second monumental epiphany. His city—his home—was nothing more than a dot below him. Everything he knew was fragile and could be destroyed; the things that mattered to him were of little value to society at large. And even his life, his own existence, was essentially meaningless, invisible when viewed from this faraway perspective. Christopher could disappear—be gone forever—and the universe would continue on unchanged. If someone else were sitting in his seat, nothing would be different. He inspected the other passengers, who casually leafed through newspapers aboard the flying, aluminum projectile. They were all ludicrously insignificant, strangers, remarkably unremarkable. Suddenly he felt very sick.

"You too?" someone asked.

"What?" said Christopher.

"Would you also like some water?" the flight attendant clarified.

"Yes, please," said Christopher, doubly relieved for the refreshment and the knowledge that no one was reading his mind.

He took a sip of water and tapped the little screen on the seat in front of him. Four movies, a layover in New York, thirty-nine games of virtual miniature golf, seven bags of peanuts, four trips to the bathroom, just one filled vomit bag, one and a half books, and twelve minutes of sleep later, Christopher arrived at Marseille Provence Airport. His visit there was at best a blur; he held his father's hand as the pair shuffled through customs and the baggage claim. They then hopped into a taxi and drove off. Anthony handed the driver an address on a piece of paper, while Christopher immediately began to hibernate.

* * *

"We're here, Christopher," said Anthony, tapping his son on the shoulder. He paid the driver a substantial amount of money—they had driven quite far—and then more or less dragged the semiconscious Christopher out of the taxi. The two of them entered a white government office with columns at the front, making their way through the lobby toward a female receptionist. Anthony began talking to her in French, which he'd picked up from Isabelle. Before long, he and Christopher found themselves navigating narrow hallways, following a nameless man in a suit.

All Christopher knew was that they were in France to meet someone, so he had no idea why they had come to this fancy building. The trio continued on for what seemed like an hour, passing by countless cubicles, corridors, and conference rooms abuzz with other suited bureaucrats. Eventually, they came to a room with a black sign above it. The man nodded at Anthony, then opened the door.

Inside, a boy a little older than Christopher sat assembling a vehicle out of plastic bricks. He was dressed in dark clothes: tennis shoes, jeans, and a tee shirt. Upon seeing his guests, the boy stood up and walked toward them.

"This is your cousin," Anthony said, turning toward his son.

"My name is Christopher Wilson," he said politely. "It's a pleasure to meet you." He had been practicing that line the entire plane ride.

"Hi," replied the boy with only a slight French accent. "I'm Arthur."

Chapter XII
Relative

Christopher and Arthur sat together, constructing toy spaceships destined to explore the distant realm of their imaginations. Christopher attached the final engine onto the back of his craft, and then looked up at his cousin. Arthur's vessel was stunningly detailed, equipped with enough firepower to blow away Christopher's shuttle as if it were indeed made of plastic. And while Christopher had incorporated bright orange and purple blocks, Arthur had used exclusively black pieces. Christopher's was creative and interesting, but ultimately harmless. Arthur's was armored and intimidating, ready for battle. Christopher was thoroughly impressed.

It was hard to believe that they were related. Their backgrounds and personalities contrasted diametrically, while their connection was the unlikely result of utter randomness. Had Anthony not sat down next to Isabelle all those years ago, Christopher would never have met Arthur. For that matter, he wouldn't even exist. Christopher lost himself in thought, marveling at the arbitrary nature of the universe.

"Hey," said Arthur, interrupting Christopher's contemplation. "Check it out." He held up his finished ship and pretended that it was flying around the room. The final product was almost twice as big as before, meaning that what Christopher had seen earlier was just one of several components.

"That's amazing," said Christopher.

"Thanks." Arthur examined his cousin's creation. "I really like yours."

"You must really like garbage, then." Christopher laughed. "How do you speak such good English?"

"I've been learning for pretty much my whole life. My mom was bilingual, and she made sure to talk to me in both languages."

"My mom spoke perfect English too," said Christopher. "I guess it's a family thing."

"Spoke?" repeated Arthur.

"Yeah. She died a while back."

"Oh, I'm sorry. My mom never even told me she had a sister, so I didn't know. That sucks, man."

"I'm over it," he said dismissively. He didn't want Arthur thinking he was the sensitive type.

"I miss my mom," said Arthur, surprising Christopher. He hadn't thought this hardened creature capable of such emotion. "She was really nice. She did lots of drugs—cocaine, heroin—just about anything she could get her hands on. Sometimes she would do things when she was high that..." He lowered his gaze for a moment. "But anyway, she was a good mother."

Christopher was not persuaded, but rather than saying so he simply nodded his head. "How'd she die?"

"She overdosed last week," said Arthur dolefully. "I knew it was going to happen one day. I just wish she'd have done it later."

"Where's your dad?" asked Christopher genuinely, forgetting his blasé pretensions.

"He left before I was born," Arthur said. "Probably out of fear. I'm alone now."

Christopher was grief-stricken. He didn't know what to say. "Jesus is always with you," he advised eventually, pointing to his cross necklace.

"My mother once said that Jesus isn't real. He's just a tool used to control people."

Christopher quickly became defensive. "Jesus *is* real. My mom told me so. Haven't you heard about the Bible?"

"Just because your mom told you something doesn't mean it's true."

"Ditto," said Christopher. "Your mom was a drug addict."

Arthur was silent.

"I'm so sorry," said Christopher. "I didn't—"

"No, it's my fault," Arthur interjected. "I shouldn't have said anything." He paused. "I don't know. Maybe God does exist. It's just really hard to have faith, you know? With all of this shit happening. They're making me see these therapists. All they say is 'everything happens for a reason' and 'God has a plan.' If that's true, I don't like the plan. Screw the plan." He was getting progressively louder, like a train coming into the station.

"The plan is why your mom died. The plan is why my parents are gone. The plan is why I'm here in this goddamn room building this crap." He picked up his spaceship and threw it down. It shattered completely, though he clearly didn't care. "I'm just tired of all the bullshit. That's all it is. School, religion, government: it's all just shit."

Christopher looked at Arthur with profound admiration. That was the most incredible thing he'd ever heard.

"I'm sorry," Arthur said. "I mean, here I am talking about this deep stuff and we've only just met."

"No, it's fine," said Christopher, completely ditching his fake persona. "We *are* technically cousins."

Arthur laughed. "Yeah, I guess we are."

"We're so different," said Christopher honestly.

"It's all relative, though. Inside, you and I are basically the same." Christopher was now totally in awe. Underneath his dark exterior, Arthur was extremely perceptive. Maybe they were related after all.

Chapter XIII
Eden

After about an hour, Anthony returned to the room, carrying a large stack of paperwork. "How's it going?" he asked.

Christopher and Arthur looked at each other. "Good," they said in unison.

"Are you guys ready to leave?"

"Where are we going, Dad?"

"I figured we'd go to Aix-en-Provence and then drive to the beach, assuming we still have the energy. Now that we're here, we might as well enjoy ourselves."

"Can Arthur come?"

Anthony smiled. "Of course," he said. "All right, let's go."

Yet another official-looking man escorted the three of them to the exit. They hopped into a cab and headed off to the city.

* * *

Anthony, Arthur, and Christopher meandered through Aix-en-Provence, taking in the smell of cheese and baguettes. Arthur spotted a novelty store and called Christopher over.

"Go ahead," said Anthony. "I'll be there soon." He waved the boys goodbye and then wandered off the main road, letting himself get lost in the world. Ambling through the avenues, he listened to vendors shout out their products in French. "Poire!" "Haricots verts!" "Fromage!" He sighed contentedly. He spent far too much time worrying, instead of living in the present, instead of taking in the moment.

Suddenly, he saw it. Nothing else was like before—the once tranquil courtyard had transformed into a busy marketplace—but the oak tree still stood: unchanged, eternal, divine. A flood of emotions rushed into Anthony's soul and drowned out his reason. The water began pouring from his eyes, unable to be contained.

Isabelle was there in a flash—the fairy materialized under the tree of life. Anthony slowly walked over to her, entirely spellbound, his face wet with memories. In the commotion no one noticed the man staring at the tree; the ordinary often disguises the extraordinary.

Anthony sat down under the shady branches, watching the leaves fly by. Isabelle sat watching as well, her pastel complexion as beautiful as ever. He could see her so vividly: her hair flowing in the soft breeze, her white shoes lying next to her delicate bare feet. After thirteen evanescent years, she was still sitting right there. Anthony decided he had either just died or been born anew, for certainly nothing so magnificent could ever have existed in his previous state of being.

* * *

Tiring of the novelty store, the boys left in search of food. Unfortunately, as they discovered several minutes into their hunt, neither of them had any money. Arthur told Christopher not to worry. He walked into a small bakery and snaked through the crowd, with the clueless Christopher following along. Lying on the countertop was a lone croissant, steaming and shimmering with a thin layer of butter.

Arthur glanced around casually. One of the store clerks was eyeing him with suspicion, but she turned away when he looked at her. After about ten seconds of idleness, he snatched the croissant and sprinted off, with Christopher running behind him in disbelief. The pair scuffled back into the store, skidding into a flower-lined area behind a garden gnome.

"Yeah!" said Arthur. "That was fun, right?"

Christopher was stunned. "What the hell, man? We could've gotten caught."

"That's part of the thrill of it," said Arthur.

"Not for me!"

"Relax. We weren't going to get caught. I have a lot of experience with this kind of thing. Besides, no one would believe you stole anything with that stupid smile of yours." He laughed.

"Still, why risk it?"

Arthur shrugged. "These are freaking great," he said, taking a bite of the croissant. "Here, try some."

"No way, man. Stealing is wrong."

"What is right and wrong, though?" said Arthur, the quintessence of moral relativity. "I'll tell you what it is. It's a concept that powerful people made up to keep everyone else in line. That way they can sleep soundly at night, on top of their stacks of money, without worrying whether their fortunes will still be there in the morning. But how did they get rich in the first place? From the blood, sweat, and tears of their employees, no doubt. Now *that's* stealing. Personally, I ignore all that stuff and look out for myself. Survival of the fittest, you know?"

Christopher pondered this reasoning. His forehead was hot and sweaty, casting off solar flares as he questioned his most deeply held values. "I don't know," he said finally.

"Exactly," said Arthur. "You don't know. I don't know. Even the president doesn't know. That's the real secret of life: nobody knows anything. People act so sure of themselves, but no one has any idea what the hell they're doing. Everyone's just guessing. And that fact that we're aware of that makes our guesses better than theirs."

"It just doesn't seem fair," said Christopher. "Taking someone else's stuff."

"Don't talk to me about fairness," said Arthur. "Both of our mothers are dead. Is that fair? There are people out there with billions of dollars just because their great-grandfathers owned horrible factories, where poor immigrants got their arms and legs chopped off working for pennies a day. These rich bastards buy exotic vacation homes they'll never live in and stock fresh beluga caviar they'll never eat, while all around them little kids are homeless and starving. Is that fair?"

"Well—"

"Look," Arthur continued. "It's a cold, unfeeling universe out there. There's no reason behind anything, which is why I do whatever I want. Sure, there are times to follow the rules and play along. But there are also times to steal shit and run. That was one of those times.

Christopher couldn't argue with this cosmic logic. Instead, he grabbed the croissant from Arthur's hand, hesitantly brought it up to his mouth, and tasted of the forbidden fruit. It was quite delicious, though whether he enjoyed the buttery dough or the sweet satisfaction of theft was unclear.

Arthur watched him, very pleased. "We're going to get along just fine," he said. "You and I are going to expose all these rules and limitations for what they really are: bullshit. You and me, man."

Christopher smiled nervously. He just liked the croissant.

Chapter XIV
Home

White-crested waves rolled onto the rocky beach—rushing in and out, in and out, in and out—forever and always. Paltry pebbles, simple stones, and massive monoliths were all worn thinner and thinner by the endless tides. Soon they would be identical, equally and entirely eroded away into nothingness. And the agent of their demise? This ultimate equalizer? Ironically, it is water—the molecular embodiment of life itself—that transforms the beastliest boulders into mere grains among the sands of time.

Christopher was lying atop those very grains when he had his third epiphany. Even if he someday realized his dreams, his legacy would nevertheless be submerged into the depths of history, lost below countless waves of progress. The tides of the universe gradually wear the extraordinary thinner and thinner, until inevitably everything erodes away into nothingness.

Arthur meanwhile waded through a web of floating seaweed. Foamy currents splashed against his neck, and then fell back down to his chest. He looked around. Dozens of people encircled him, laughing and playing with their families. Arthur watched them enviously. He had no father, no mother, no grandparents. Never again would he look into someone's eyes and see his roots.

An abandoned wooden boat glided past him, receding ever farther from the beach. With nothing left to tie him down, Arthur felt his feet rise up from the ocean floor and break through the surface. Sprawled supine atop the waves, he stared at the Mediterranean sun, allowing its heat to melt away his icy thoughts. He was now completely under nature's control, having given up fighting against the tireless tides. Soon he too began floating away from the shore, following the boat into the sea, adrift.

Anthony had only just stepped into the water when he saw Arthur, who was now approaching the buoys that marked the edge of the swimming area. He immediately headed over to his nephew, using his arms to propel himself against the flow. The sea rapidly became too deep to walk with any speed, so he began swimming to Arthur, his arms lunging forward with swift, powerful strokes. After no more than two minutes he was there, treading water at the rope dividing humanity and the wild.

"Are you all right, Arthur?" he called out, trying to mask his parental concern.

Upon hearing the voice, Arthur awakened from his conscious trance. "I'm fine," he murmured eventually.

"Let's get you back," said Anthony, grabbing Arthur with one hand while battling the undertow with the other.

"I'm fine," Arthur repeated to himself.

Anthony kept going. "I've got you," he said, dragging the boy back to civilization. "I've got you."

* * *

Anthony reviewed the mountain of papers from the government office, his trembling digits rendering the text illegible. This is what Isabelle would've wanted, he told himself. This was the right thing to do. He turned toward Arthur, who was shoveling sand onto Christopher's feet.

"Boys, I have some news," he stuttered, ending a lengthy period of silence.

"What is it, Dad?"

"Well..." he trailed off, searching for the right words. Nothing in his life could have prepared him for this situation. "You guys seem to be having a good time," he said finally. "I don't know. What are you thinking, Arthur?"

"Yeah, today's been great, Mr. Wilson," he said honestly.

"Please, call me Uncle Anthony, or just Anthony, or—well, call me whatever you want."

"Sure thing, Uncle Anthony."

"Anyway, the reason we're here in France is that we're your closest relations, Arthur. And given that, we want to make sure that you're taken care of, which is why…" he stammered, "why…why you're going to come live with me and Christopher in Seattle." He breathed out heavily and waited for a reaction.

"Cool," Arthur said with baffling composure. He had more or less arrived at that conclusion already.

Christopher on the other hand was completely dismayed. "Really, Dad?" he asked.

"Really, buddy."

"Awesome!" Christopher looked at Arthur giddily. "Can you believe it?" he said. "We're like brothers now!"

"Brothers," Arthur affirmed, before shifting into a deeply pensive state. Seattle, he mused. It was rainy there. And so far away; so vastly different. Then again, he was sick of France—too many painful memories. Arthur looked out into the water. The ocean here was the same as the one in Seattle; fish probably swam back and forth all the time.

Meanwhile, Anthony was delighted that his announcement had been so well received. He felt a tremendous sense of closure, as if this trip were the final stage of mourning for his wife. Everything was falling into place: his job, his family, his psyche. His exhalations echoed the crashing waves as his body harmonized with the rhythm of the world.

* * *

Arthur pointed toward a small blue house. "C'est là-bas," he said.

The taxi driver nodded and pulled over. "Voilà."

"Attendez ici," directed Arthur. One by one, he and the Wilsons exited the cab.

"Merci," said Anthony.

"Merci," said Arthur.

"Mur-see," mimicked Christopher.

The house was, in a word, scary. The windows were barred, broken, and boarded up, and the steps leading to the door were cracked and uneven. It was hardly an inviting entrance, though to be fair, no amount of refurbishment could mask the house's deeply rooted decay. Its very essence was dark and dreary and dead.

Over the course of a lifetime, people experience literally thousands of places: homes, schools, zoos, amusement parks, stores, restaurants, movie theaters, churches, stadiums, dorm rooms, office buildings, gyms, museums, golf courses, retirement facilities, hospitals, cemeteries. Some of these places are frequented on a daily basis, others more rarely, and many just once or twice. Yet for each and every place, there is a final visit, a last memory that is either forgotten or taken to the grave. Ordinarily, people ignore the chance that they may never return to their present locale, choosing to move forward rather than dwell in the past. And for good reason: otherwise relentless nostalgia would prevent them from accomplishing anything worthwhile. But every so often, people are forced to confront the fact that what they see now they will never see again, that what is and has always been will be no more.

Arthur entered his former dwelling and came to a halt, his legs weighted down by the finality of the moment. Inside, the foyer was illuminated only by crisscrossing beams of light that poked through the perforated ceiling. The moldy floorboards creaked loudly with every movement, while the air was musty and hot. Arthur smiled. He was home.

Anthony and Christopher followed along nervously. What were sentimental relics to Arthur were alien discards to the Wilsons. Anthony wandered off to the kitchen, where a dozen beers stood half-empty on the counter. He opened the refrigerator. It smelled like rotten death, and he slammed it shut so hard that it nearly toppled over.

Christopher continued down a hallway until he reached Arthur's room. Posters of metal bands and French models were taped along the walls haphazardly, while clothes and candy wrappers littered the filthy carpet. Christopher reflected on his own bedroom back in Seattle, with its tidy cabinets and labeled shelves. I'll never be as cool as Arthur, he lamented.

Arthur himself was sitting on his favorite thing in the whole house: a black chair—upholstered in surprisingly upscale velvet—that rested in front of an old writing desk. Whenever his mom got really high, he would go into the den, lock the door, and curl up on its soft fabric. As soon as he closed his eyes, he suddenly found himself in Paris or London or Rome, walking down a bustling boulevard with an ice cream cone in his hand, watching carefree people exchanging pleasantries under sunlit café awnings.

But now, Arthur's eyes were wide open. He looked at his backyard for the last time through a grayed window, no longer able to escape from reality. His face was cast in shadows as he left his old life behind.

Chapter XV
Blood

For as long as he could remember, Christopher had been playing daily basketball against his father, and on each occasion he had come in second. According to Christopher's estimation, his all-time record now stood at zero wins to six hundred eighty-nine losses, although the real standings were even more one-sided. But such prolonged failure had fueled Christopher's fire, and on this late summer afternoon, the student finally had his master on the brink of defeat.

Anthony didn't believe in going easy on his son. In principle, he was trying to teach Christopher perseverance, sportsmanship, and ambition. In reality, he simply hated to lose. Victory had been a foregone conclusion for most of their games, with Anthony's height advantage alone proving insurmountable. But for at least a year now, the competition had been steadily intensifying, with Arthur around to help Christopher improve. At this point, the fifteen-year-old Frenchman was merely practice fodder for the thirteen-year-old prodigy, but the hours of driveway scrimmaging were productive nonetheless.

Anthony wiped the sweat off his forehead and panted with exhaustion. He had taken the early lead, per usual, by backing Christopher down with his superior size. Christopher was no longer the little boy he had once been, however, and he was now only four inches shorter than his father. Every movement was a struggle, with the old veteran absorbing elbow after elbow to the ribs while plowing his way to the basket. The incessant pounding had worn Anthony out, while Christopher bounced around with impossible energy, gradually rallying to shrink the deficit.

Arthur looked on from the grass, drinking a can of soda, mildly amused. "You look like you need a break," he said dispassionately, "and maybe a doctor too." He would never understand why the naturally cerebral Wilsons resorted to such savagery during these games, nor could he ever join their exclusive bloodline. For better or worse, Arthur was an outcast. Anthony meanwhile leaned over and caught his breath, holding the ball against his dripping bare chest.

"Let's go," said Christopher with belligerent concentration. Anthony dribbled up slowly, turned his back to the rim, and then spun left. Christopher was already waiting there to meet him, causing Anthony, who had been caught off guard by the capable defense, to accidentally shoulder his son in the mouth. Christopher began bleeding, his teeth having punctured his gums.

"I'm sorry, buddy," Anthony said. "Are you okay?"

"I'm fine," replied Christopher, spitting out red.

"Well, you certainly are tough. That was a foul. It's your ball."

Christopher removed his shirt and cleaned himself up. The two of them looked less like basketball players and more like gladiators: bloody and bruised, sweating under the evening sun, eyes fixed intently on each other's movements.

Christopher casually threw the ball between his legs, behind his back, and into his palm. He heaved the ball up, but Anthony effortlessly blocked it into the garage door. He should have known better than to use his father's own move against him.

"I guess your dad can still play a little bit," Anthony said. He picked up the ball and drove to the hoop, charging forward like an incensed bull. Christopher expertly stepped aside, giving Anthony the impression that the path was clear. Then, just as he was about to shoot, Christopher reached in from behind and snatched the ball out of his father's hands.

"So can I," countered Christopher, dribbling to the crack that served as the three-point line. He let loose a long shot that swished perfectly through the net. When he was alone, he didn't miss from there. He cared too much not to make it.

"Nice," praised Anthony. "I have to get closer and not let you shoot that."

Christopher sprinted after the ball, not wanting to give his opponent a chance to rest. Anthony crowded his son to prevent another three-pointer, allowing Christopher to dart past him for a difficult, soaring finger-roll.

"Better not get too close," advised Christopher smugly. At that moment, something deep within Anthony was triggered, and new life flowed through his veins. From then on, neither player scored for over ten minutes. What began as a friendly basketball contest had become a life-and-death duel between experience and youth. Only as the sun dipped below the horizon did Christopher earn another point, finally completing his gutsy comeback.

"Tie game," Arthur called out. "Nineteen to nineteen. Whoever makes the next shot wins."

Neither Anthony nor Christopher heard him. For them, nothing existed beyond the concrete driveway. Into the night they played, with the stars and the streetlights shimmering on their sweaty skins, the court only barely visible, and the match thrown into stalemate once more. Dribbling and shooting had been rendered irrelevant—only sheer grit would end this epic showdown.

What Christopher lacked in size, he made up for with stamina. The latter ultimately proved decisive, as Christopher willed his way to the hoop, jumped up with all his strength, and put the ball in for the victory. Father and son wobbled over to the grass and collapsed.

"Nice job, dude," said Arthur, heading inside.

Christopher smiled weakly, the only gesture of which he was currently capable.

"Good game, Dad," he said eventually.

"You too, buddy," wheezed Anthony. The pair looked up at the night sky. Above them, a star shone with unrivaled brilliance, separating itself from the others.

"I'll never be able to beat you again, will I?" Anthony said, before turning around to vomit.

Chapter XVI
Her

Christopher carefully scrutinized his reflection, frowning with disapproval. He looked really young—too young for the ninth grade. He walked into the kitchen, where Arthur was wolfing down a bowl of cereal, and poured himself a glass of orange juice. Arthur dropped his spoon and stared at his cousin.

"What?" Christopher demanded.

"You look just like your dad."

Christopher remembered his mother saying the same thing when he was little. His mother. Suddenly he was stricken with sadness: he couldn't picture her face.

"Relax, man," Arthur continued. "It's biology. We all become like our parents."

Christopher regained awareness of the present. "Not me," he said.

"What's this?" asked Anthony, coming into the room.

"Good morning," said Christopher quickly.

"He said he doesn't want to be like you," snitched Arthur. Christopher shot him a frustrated look.

Anthony smiled. "In that case, you should probably stop dressing like me." He picked up a brown leather briefcase and started out the door. "C'mon boys, let's go. We can't afford to be late on the first day."

Anthony, not yet forty years old, had already suffered through a minor midlife crisis, the proof of which was parked in his garage. With extreme reverence and caution, he slid into the sleek charcoal Porsche, which despite costing him a year's salary was still the best purchase he'd ever made. Arthur claimed the passenger seat, while Christopher reluctantly crawled into the back. Anthony slammed down on the accelerator, and the trio rocketed onto the road. Christopher fidgeted nervously, fixing his hair in the rearview mirror.

"Dude, stop worrying," said Arthur. "It's your first day of high school, you're wearing a polo shirt, and your dad is the freaking principal. You're going to get killed no matter how nice your hair looks."

"Hey!" Anthony exclaimed incredulously.

"What? I'm just letting him know the truth."

"Why don't *you* get beat up?" Christopher asked. "I mean, we're basically brothers."

"Well, to begin with, I look different than you, I talk different than you, and I have a different last name than you. No one will think that we're related, and I don't want you telling people that we are."

"Jesus, Arthur, take it easy on him. He's got enough to worry about already."

"You know what you need?" said Arthur, changing the subject. "A nickname."

"Do you have a nickname?" asked Christopher dubiously.

"As a matter of fact, I do," said Arthur. He felt Anthony's interest spike and regretted saying anything.

"What is it?" probed Christopher.

"Black," he mouthed quietly.

"Black?" Anthony confirmed.

"Yeah, black," Arthur repeated. "Like my last name."

"Your last name is Noir," said Christopher.

"Noir means black in French, buddy," Anthony informed him.

"Two years living together and you still didn't know that?" Arthur teased. "I must've told you at some point. It's weird, though, because my dad's last name was Noir, which means black, and my mom's was Blanche, which means white. I could've gone either way, but I chose black. It suits me, I think."

"I don't like it," said Anthony. "It's a little too dark for my taste."

Arthur shrugged. "How about just Chris?" he said. "Christopher is so formal."

"No way," said Christopher. "I'm not messing up my name. I love my name." He looked down at his cross, its heavy chain weighting down his neck. It was a perfect fit, the cross.

"Christopher is a great name," Anthony chimed in. "Your mother was smart giving it to you."

"Whatever," said Arthur. "You're digging your own grave."

Anthony skidded into his designated parking spot and looked at Arthur. "Try not to cuss out any of your new teachers," he said. "I don't want to see you until after school."

"What if they're full of shit?" asked Arthur seriously.

"Everyone is," said Anthony. "That doesn't mean you have to tell them."

Arthur opened his door. "Au revoir," he said suavely.

"Bye," said Christopher as the door slammed shut.

Anthony addressed his son. "Don't end up like him," he said. "I know his act looks cool, but trust me, it's not worth it. One mistake can wreck your entire life."

"Don't worry, Dad," said Christopher, almost sadly. "I'm not like him."

Anthony got out of the car. "I'll walk you to your first class," he said.

"I don't think this is a good idea, Dad."

"Sure it is," said Anthony. "I wouldn't want you to get lost." Christopher followed him through an ocean of students, fighting against the tides. He vaguely recalled his first day of elementary school, feeling the same combination of fear and smallness as he had back then. Only now the school was objectively enormous, not just to the eyes of a first grader, and the principal he was following was not Mr. Henderson but Mr. Wilson.

"All right, we're here," said Anthony. "Have a good day, Christopher. I don't want to see you until the end of the day either." He laughed and then kissed his son on the head. A couple of the other kids were watching, so Christopher tried to look adult. He backed away from his father toward the classroom, inadvertently bumping into a girl.

"Sorry," he said, turning to face her.

"It's fine," she replied. Christopher hadn't seen her in more than three years. She looked much older now, with her dirty blonde hair parted neatly down the middle and her brown eyes lightly accented with makeup.

"Emily."

Chapter XVII
Solitude

Christopher sprinted past teachers and students strolling nonchalantly through the hallway. He swiveled around apprehensively, realizing that he was going to be both late and exhausted by the time he found the gymnasium. To his right, Christopher miraculously saw the old building with banners across the top. He bolted in its direction, arriving there just as the bell began to ring.

Stopping in front of the entrance, Christopher breathed in deeply and pulled on the door handle. It wouldn't budge. He pulled harder, but again his efforts were futile.

"Need some help?" inquired a tallish black man with a deep voice.

"I think it's locked," Christopher panted.

The man gently pressed the door open. "You'll figure it out eventually." He chuckled, pointing to the word "PUSH" printed in bold letters.

Christopher flushed. "I didn't see the sign," he stated obviously.

"No harm done," the man said. "You got a name?"

"Christopher."

"It's a pleasure to meet you, Christopher. You're a freshman, am I right?"

"Yeah. I'm still getting to know this place."

"Don't worry about it. I did a lot of stupid stuff when I was your age. I still do, actually." He laughed again, bending over to Christopher's level. "I'm Coach Johnson."

"Basketball Coach Johnson?"

"That's me. Are you here for the tryout?"

"Yes, sir."

"Good man. Now listen, this is a competitive team. We won the city championship last season, and the main reason was our experience. Because of that, there aren't a lot of spots for underclassmen. I bet you have talent, but don't get discouraged if you get left off the roster this year. Just keep practicing and keep growing. The sky's the limit." Christopher nodded, feeling much more relaxed. "The other guys are standing over there by the baseline."

Christopher looked at the other hopefuls. There were roughly thirty of them, all taller and more muscular than he was. Many were sporting North Valley gear, a few had on their jerseys from the previous season, and all were wearing shiny new sneakers, with the exception of an enormous blonde-haired boy in sandals. He must have been at least six-foot-nine, and he clearly wasn't concerned about his chances to stay on the team.

"Most of them couldn't make a layup to save their lives," said the coach, sensing Christopher's renewed anxiety. "Go on."

Christopher hustled over to the baseline. With his well-worn tennis shoes and red-cheeked expression, he looked more like a ball boy than a point guard.

"I didn't know they let kindergartners in this gym," jeered a thickset kid whose jawline was peppered with uneven stubble.

"C'mon, Jack, be friendly," someone said.

"Hey, I'm just having fun with him." Jack looked at Christopher. "I'm kidding, dude. We could really use you. If we ever need a spare basketball, you'd be perfect for the job."

"Shut up, man," said the blonde-haired giant.

"Why don't you shut up, Spencer?"

"Hey, hey," interjected Coach Johnson. "Let's be civil, everybody. Save that energy for the court. Jack, go run a lap. Spencer, why aren't you wearing sneakers?"

"I forgot them, Coach."

"Well bring them next time. Don't think I won't cut you just because you can change the lights without a ladder. I have time to get a ladder, what I don't have time for is you not coming prepared to play."

"It won't happen again," Spencer said.

Coach Johnson turned the other way. "Let's go, Jack!" he yelled. "I want to see those legs higher! Pump your arms!" He looked at Christopher and smiled. "Run, Jack, run!"

Jack slowly jogged around the final bend, glaring defiantly at Coach Johnson throughout.

"Now then," Coach continued, "welcome back to those of you who were on last year's team. I'd like to congratulate you all again for your terrific season." Jack held out his arms arrogantly. "I say that because from this point on, our focus is on the future and the future only. We can't rest on past accomplishments. And let me make this very clear." He looked at Jack. "Having been on that team does not mean you will make it this time. You have to prove to me that you deserve to be here."

Jack hissed loudly.

"Okay, let's start with some foul shooting. Christopher, you should take off that cross. You might get the chain caught on something."

"I can't," apologized Christopher. The other kids looked at him with confusion, while Coach Johnson nodded understandingly.

"Let's go, ladies," Coach said. "What are you all waiting for?"

* * *

Christopher stood at the free throw line. All the other players and coaches watched intently, judging him based on his every movement. Sweat dripped down his neck and onto the wood below. He spun the ball out in front of him, dribbled twice, exhaled to regain his composure, and took the shot. It landed with a thud onto the back of the rim, then bounced off the backboard and hit the floor. The pressure was unbearable, causing him to tense up and throw too forcefully.

"Four feet tall and he can't even shoot," Jack taunted from the bench. Christopher ignored him and repeated his routine, releasing the ball much more gently this time. But he had overcompensated: the shot barely grazed the front of the rim, ricocheting backward as if to mock him. Christopher shook his head: he never missed when he was alone.

"Hey, what's the deal with that scar on your face, man?" Jack persisted. "Are you some kind of freak?"

"Stop it," warned Coach Johnson.

"Chill," Jack said. "I'm just playing around."

"Well, I'm *not* playing around. Be quiet or you'll be running laps until Christmas."

"Looks like you got a friend, kid. Oh yeah, you're the principal's son, aren't you? I bet Coach will put you on the team just so he doesn't get fired."

"Enough! Don't worry about that delinquent, Christopher. Concentrate on the target."

Christopher continued to struggle. The other boys did poorly as well, which was a relief. None of them seemed nearly as disappointed as he was, and Christopher realized that he was probably more skilled than anyone there. The last up to the line was Jack, who easily swished his first nine shots, then banked in the tenth one out of boredom. No wonder he got away with bullying; he was the star of the team.

After some conditioning work and passing exercises, the players were broken up into trios for three-on-three games. Eventually, it was Christopher's turn, and unsurprisingly Jack was on the other team. Coach Johnson had strictly banned trash-talking and rough play, but Christopher nevertheless found himself battered by insults and uppercuts alike. He was the smallest person on the court, though Jack still decided to shadow him wherever he went.

Finally, Christopher got the ball, while Jack, now with an almost warlike countenance, formed an impenetrable barricade with his bulky arms. Christopher dribbled forward with his back to the basket, feeling elbows slice their way into his spine. Despite Jack's intensity and strength, however, Christopher single-mindedly advanced toward the hoop. He had survived a gladiator fight against his father, so he could handle a little physicality.

Christopher faked a shot, but Jack adroitly read the play and nearly snatched the ball. Instinctively, Christopher performed his dad's move. He whipped the ball between his legs before immediately flinging it behind his back, catching Jack completely by surprise and causing him to lose his footing. Christopher charged ahead, while Jack—who had foolishly attempted to catch up—slipped and tumbled to the ground.

The other players gasped in disbelief. But their shock quickly became concern—just as Christopher leaped for the layup, Jack grabbed his foot and yanked him down. Jack hadn't fully thought through the consequences of this move; he had acted purely out of embarrassment. Christopher meanwhile plummeted to the pitiless plywood, hitting the floor with a sickening crack. He screamed.

"Get out!" Coach Johnson shouted. Jack hustled out of the building, having lost control of the situation.

Christopher lay on his stomach with his limbs splayed out in unnatural directions, surrounded by curious onlookers.

"Back up! Back up!" hollered the coach. "Are you all right, kid?"

"I'm okay," Christopher groaned. After about a minute he got up, his face bloodied, his right leg already a disturbing shade of blue.

"You are one tough guy. Let me call your father."

"No, no," insisted Christopher. "I'll handle it." He staggered to the exit, grimacing with every step.

"Hey, don't leave," Coach called. "You shouldn't be walking on that."

But Christopher kept going. He opened the door, looking at the coach with a forced smile. As soon as it shut, he collapsed onto the asphalt, breathing in harshly while nursing his injury.

Physically and mentally incapacitated, Christopher followed the cross as it rose and fell atop his chest, its golden hue imparting spiritual import to an intrinsically material trinket. Its previous guardians were dead and buried, their piety insufficient to stop the cycle of life. Christopher would inevitably join them down there and cast off his mortal misery. For the moment, however, he suffered in solitude.

Chapter XVIII
Stranger

Christopher limped up to the locker room door, scanning the column of names. Big Spencer Davies had made the team, sandals and all, his moniker printed fittingly at the top of the page. Most of the others he didn't recognize: Kevin Feldstein, Jason Hunt, Alex Jordan. Christopher moved his finger down the paper, realizing that the list was arranged alphabetically. Marcus Lovett, Ryan Sanders, Quentin Stevens— faceless strangers filling up the precious spots.

At the very bottom, where his name should have been, was the most infuriating thing that Christopher had ever seen. Jack Thomas, who was directly responsible for the brace wrapped around his leg, had not only taken his place on the roster but had been selected as the team captain. Christopher stared at the capital letter "C" adjacent to the bully's name, unassailable proof that divine providence was no match for satanic irony. Despite Coach Johnson's righteous aura, he ostensibly valued talent over principle, for he had crowned the devil himself. Christopher sighed. He had lost many times in his life, but never before had he failed.

The drive home that afternoon was painfully silent. Anthony had spent his day dealing with parents who were livid at their children's teachers, and was in no mood for conversation. Arthur was listening to rap music via needlessly expensive headphones, moving his hand to the beat. Christopher rested his head against the window, lamenting the absurdity of the universe. The car pulled into the garage, and the three of them entered the house without a word.

Christopher walked into his room, for no particular reason. There was nothing meaningful about it—no purpose or direction. In fact, he wasn't sure why he did anything, other than to maintain his routine. Perhaps people only exist out of habit, losing touch with reality the moment they acknowledge the staggering insignificance of their lives.

Arthur noticed Christopher lying on his bed, clearly perturbed. "What's up, man?" he said, removing his flashy headgear.

Christopher snapped out of his trance. He thought for a second, and then said confidently, "Everything is bullshit."

Arthur was surprised: he'd never heard Christopher curse before. Christopher was equally surprised: he'd never head himself curse either.

"I totally agree," Arthur said. "I'm glad you're with me, finally."

"'You and I are going to expose all these rules and limitations for what they really are,'" Christopher quoted.

"Did I say that?"

"Yeah, when we first met."

"That was a rough time for me. I might have overstated things a bit."

"No, you were exactly right, and I'm in. You and me, man." Christopher looked at Arthur—his only friend in the world—and pondered the preposterous serendipity that had brought them together. Arthur looked back at Christopher, mildly concerned.

* * *

Anthony tore open the envelope and slowly unfolded Arthur's report card, preparing himself for the worst. He frowned. It was indeed the worst.

"Two C's, two D's, and an F," he read out incredulously. "Arthur, you're way too smart to be doing so poorly."

"Hey, don't forget my A in French," said Arthur.

"You're from France!" Anthony exclaimed. "The only reason you're even in that class is because otherwise you'd be failing everything."

Arthur shrugged.

"You should start taking an interest in your future," said Anthony. "If I wasn't the principal, you'd be stuck repeating sophomore year.

"Just what this country needs: another corrupt bureaucrat." Arthur left the room.

"What am I going to do with him?" Anthony moaned.

Christopher shrugged, mimicking his cousin.

"What's up with you?"

"I don't know," said Christopher casually.

Anthony shook his head, then proceeded to open Christopher's report card. "All A's again," he said. "It's such a relief having one easy kid."

Christopher rolled his eyes and left the room.

"What the hell am I doing wrong?" Anthony wondered aloud. He looked at himself in the mirror that hung above the kitchen table. His once black hair had turned gray with stress, or perhaps with submission. Soon it would be white, and the transformation would be finished. He whirled around, unable to stand his reflection any longer. Had he really just scolded Arthur over his grades? Inside, he still felt like a teenager, still viewed himself as a rebel battling to overthrow the establishment. But on the outside he looked old, stern, and authoritative. He needed some hair dye.

* * *

Christopher sat down next to his cousin, opening up *The Stranger* by Albert Camus. It was Arthur's favorite book—he owned copies in both English and the original French—and his entire outlook on life was rooted in its pages. Because Christopher now shared that outlook, he was ready to read the manifesto.

"Aujourd'hui, Maman est morte," said Arthur, reciting the novel's first line from memory.

Christopher looked down at his translated version. "Mother died today," he said. The boys looked at each other with a mutual empathy beyond the bounds of language.

"Keep reading," prodded Arthur.

Christopher sighed loudly and then continued. "Or, maybe, yesterday; I can't be sure." He paused. How could this character not know when his own mother died? And why didn't he seem to care?

"What are you thinking?" asked Arthur.

"Why didn't he love his mom?"

"Who says he didn't? I think he loved her a lot."

"Well, he certainly isn't acting like it. He seems so...cold."

"Maybe he learned to accept life and not wallow in self-pity."

"But his mom *died*," Christopher emphasized. "We both know how bad that feels."

"I'm not saying that it's easy to move on when you lose someone close to you, because obviously it's not. But it is an ideal to strive for, and it's something that I work on every day." He waited for a response, and then tried a different tack. "Consider this, Christopher: everyone that's ever lived is dead or will be soon, and all the people that ever will live are gonna die too. Dying is natural. You're gonna die. I'm gonna die. We're all gonna die someday. And it's that knowledge that makes me feel alive."

"Very comforting," said Christopher sarcastically.

"It can be. Once you recognize that nothing really *means* anything, you understand that death is just another thing that happens. So why would you waste the short time you have on earth being depressed about it?"

"I guess you're right. I just can't ignore my sadness sometimes."

"Yes, you can. And trust me: life is much less stressful if you stop fighting against the universe."

* * *

Christopher read *The Stranger* until he was too tired to go on, at which point he closed the book and placed it on top of his Bible. One was the definitive guide to morality, while the other was entirely fiction.

Chapter XIX
Fusion

A lone bead of sweat trickled down Christopher's neck and onto his moist shirt. The science classroom was rapidly becoming insufferable, the ancient air conditioner having lost its battle against the sweltering autumn heat.

"Can anyone tell me how stars generate energy?" asked Mr. Adams. It was an appropriate question for the day. Christopher raised his hand, out of habit more than anything else.

"Yes, Christopher?"

"Stars fuse hydrogen atoms into helium atoms," he said, "which is the source of their power."

"Very good," said Mr. Adams.

Christopher desperately tried to stop talking, but his efforts proved unsuccessful. "Except once a star runs out of hydrogen, it starts fusing together heavier elements," he said. "People are mostly just carbon, oxygen, and nitrogen, which were all made in dying stars."

"Wow. Someone knows their astronomy." Mr. Adams turned around and began writing on the board.

"Smart-ass," someone said, inciting muffled laughter across the room.

Christopher closed his eyes, embarrassed by his genius. He simultaneously sensed everything happening in the room: chalk scraping against the blackboard, classmates chewing gum while exchanging notes, the subtle smell of perspiration gathering above the chairs. Disillusioned as he was, Christopher could not ignore the chemicals in his brain; he could not break free from the physical and emotional sensations that weighted him down to reality. Why couldn't he be more like Arthur?

"Be quiet, everyone," called Mr. Adams. "We haven't done any projects yet, so today all of you are going to model stars using the posters behind me. That way it'll look like you learned something when your parents come in here next week." He laughed. "Let's do this in pairs, actually. Kevin, you'll work with Samantha. Alexis, you'll partner with Mark. Christopher, you'll be with Emily…"

Christopher gulped. He'd been avoiding Emily for more than a year now, over which time he'd built up a mental barrier that made him nervous just looking at her. Emily meanwhile walked gracefully over to Christopher's desk and pulled up a chair.

"Oh yeah," she said. "I'm definitely gonna ace this assignment." She smiled at Christopher, who quickly looked away. "Hey, I've been meaning to ask you: are you mad at me? We haven't really talked at all this year."

Christopher's eyes darted back up and met hers. "Of course not," he said.

"Okay, good. I mean, we've known each other for a while, and you seem like the same nice guy from before."

"Nah, I've changed."

Emily thought for a moment. "Well, I do still want to be friends, if it's all right with you."

"Yeah, sure," Christopher said coolly. He gazed across the desk at Emily's jean jacket and silver earrings. "I'll take care of this," he said, pointing to the poster. Emily smiled. Christopher smiled. Suddenly he was transported back to the first grade, sitting at the table in the corner of Mrs. Wright's room. This is going to be great, he thought.

The bell rang just as Christopher finished drawing the star's photosphere. The other kids hurried out of the classroom and into the open air, happy to be heading home. Christopher was not so fortunate: he still had practice to attend. He passed through the door and glanced at Emily, who walked beside him.

"Bye," he said.

"Bye," she echoed warmly.

Christopher turned toward the gym, supremely content. He took several strides in that direction and then looked back at Emily. She was beautiful, with her blonde hair shimmering in the afternoon light. Just then, a boy wearing tight black jeans and a tattered tee shirt approached her with his arms extended. She embraced him tightly, while he gently caressed her neck and kissed her glossy lips. Christopher watched in disbelief—it was Arthur.

* * *

Sunlight flamed down from the heavens, melting through the metal handle with its molten rays. Christopher rested his fingers on the grip, allowing the brass to singe his skin, absorbing its solar scintillance. His arms glowed with a reddish blaze that burned not from the external light but from his inner inferno. The individual fibers of his muscles tightened with readiness as he opened the gymnasium door, remembering to push. For the first time in a very long while, he felt alive—acutely aware of his physical power.

Christopher had performed spectacularly during his second round of tryouts, and this time he had easily made the team. Despite his standout ability, however, Christopher was still just a sophomore, which secured him a permanent place on the bench. And although he had grown two inches over the summer, he was nevertheless the runt of the roster. Meanwhile, Jack, now a six-foot-three, two-hundred-pound senior, had become a semi-celebrity in Seattle. Several schools had already offered him full scholarships, but he was holding out for better prospects.

"All right, let's start off with a layup drill," said Coach Johnson, his hairline having receded slightly since the previous fall. Christopher scurried over to the top of the key. Half of his teammates took turns attempting ridiculous, flailing shots, while the other half waited for the rebound. Christopher joined the rebounding line and stood under the rim.

Jack, spotting his nemesis in a vulnerable position, dribbled toward the basket and threw down a vengeful dunk. Screaming with primal rage, he stared down menacingly at Christopher. Christopher glared back, pulsating with heliacal energy that was barely restrained by his youthful ethics.

The practice continued like this for about an hour, with Jack slowly wearing away Christopher's patience. Every time he would touch the ball, Jack would yell something about his size or his skinniness or his scar. When he made a shot, he was lucky; when he missed, he was garbage, a useless waste of resources. Each time he tried to move, Jack's elbows and knees jabbed his broiling body. Christopher gradually shed the last of his tolerance, his raw emotion rising to the surface, his nostrils steaming with fiery anger.

Christopher was pursuing the opposing point guard when Jack leveled him with an illegal screen. Lying on the ground, he looked up the bully, who was spitting out profane declarations of his dominance. Christopher stood up as quickly as he could and walked away, fuming.

"Yeah, that's right, run home," taunted Jack. "Go and cry to your principal daddy."

"Jack," warned Coach Johnson.

But Jack didn't stop. "Tell your mother that I'm coming for her next."

Christopher's eyes narrowed, his fists clenched, and his teeth grinded together. He suddenly turned around and punched Jack squarely in the jaw, with the pent up force of a thousand other punches he'd held back. That single blow sent Jack careening toward midcourt, his mouth mutilated and badly bleeding. Christopher examined his hand. It was bloody as well, but he felt no pain. The other players watched in stunned silence as Christopher smiled. No longer would he be called a nerd, or a brainiac, or a dweeb. Now he was dangerous, volatile, bad.

"Get out!" commanded Coach Johnson, just as he had directed Jack a year ago. Christopher nodded and ambled out of practice. He opened the door, licking the blood off of his knuckles. For most of his life, he had been trapped, imprisoned by the chains of expectations. But with one punch he'd broken loose—free from his fear of disappointing other people. Christopher beamed under the hot sun. At long last, he had escaped.

Chapter XX
Box

Jack glared savagely at Christopher, his face visibly misshapen. Christopher looked away, reading the gold nameplate on his father's desk over and over again. "Principal Wilson." "Principal Wilson." "Principal Wilson." It never changed, nor could it. The letters were engraved immutably, carved into the annals of history forevermore. Doctor Wilson, Father Wilson, President Wilson: roads that had long ago veered prohibitively far from the path that his father followed.

"All right, so what happened?" Anthony asked.

"He punched me for no freaking reason," Jack replied, scowling at Christopher.

"You must have done something," said Anthony. "It doesn't excuse his actions, which were unacceptable. But I know my son, and he's never even thought about hurting anybody. C'mon, level with me, one man to another. What did you say that made him hit you?"

"Nothing," Jack lied unflinchingly. He had a lot of practice with massaging the truth.

"Christopher," said Anthony. "I want to hear your side of the story. What happened?"

Christopher thought for a long time, his gaze darting from his father to his foe. In both of them, he saw himself. Down both roads, he saw a future. Here the two roads split, and the choice was his to make. He could explain that Jack had started everything, that he had threatened his dead mother. Or he could shoulder the blame, so that Jack and all the others like him would know he was their equal.

"Christopher?"

"I hit him," he said finally. "I didn't like him. I still don't like him. So I hit him."

Anthony watched his son's blue eyes darken beneath his black hair. Christopher was shaking on the inside, regretting his choice. On the outside, though, he was steady.

"Okay, Jack," said Anthony. "I'm going to let you go. Get out of here."

"Let me go?" Jack quoted indignantly. "I'm the goddamn victim."

"Sure you are," said Anthony. "Now leave." Jack shook his head and stormed out. Anthony sighed.

"So how long am I suspended?" asked Christopher flatly.

"I don't know, buddy. I don't know. Is there anything you want to tell me now that Jack's gone?"

"No."

"Well, I can't say that I never misbehaved when I was a kid, and I can tell Jack must've said something to get you that riled up. I mean, you absolutely decked him." Anthony felt something like pride stirring in his veins, but he quickly regained his mature demeanor. He rested his head on his hand for about a minute. "Given what I've heard—or, really, what I haven't heard—I have no choice but to suspend you for one week."

Christopher blinked indifferently, while Anthony walked through his office and closed the door.

"I love you, Son," he said, kneeling down and wrapping his arms around Christopher's chest. "This doesn't change that. Nothing will ever change that. I will love you whether you want me to or not. I know high school can be rough, and I know you're under a lot of pressure. But don't lose yourself and who you are trying to handle it." Christopher struggled to remain inexpressive.

"You're better than that idiot Jack," Anthony continued. "You're better than all these kids. Take this week to sort things out, read some books, whatever. You'll come back good as new."

Christopher abruptly rose to his feet. "Let's go home," he said stoically.

Anthony smiled and reached for his car keys. Christopher was by far his favorite student—maybe he was a corrupt bureaucrat after all.

* * *

A gray Porsche shot into the movie theater parking lot, screaming past frightened pedestrians. Fluorescent signs illuminated the cinema entrance, but neither stars nor streetlights shined at the back. The Porsche opted for darkness, wildly swerving between the two lanes. To be fair, it was the driver's first time behind the wheel of this particular vehicle. He was—as he likely would have put it—borrowing the car for the night. He was also rather high, though that was hardly newsworthy.

The car thankfully skidded to a halt. In the passenger seat, Emily let out a long sigh of relief: it had been a terrifying ride. To her left, Arthur clumsily dug through his pocket and pulled out a white, circular pill. He'd gotten it all the way up to his mouth before Emily reached over to stop him.

"You want this?" asked Arthur. "It's pretty intense."

"You know I don't do that," Emily said. "I just think you've had enough."

"I haven't puked," said Arthur seriously.

"So it's a good time to stop, then."

"What's wrong, babe?" Arthur gracelessly put his hands on her legs. "Don't you like this car?"

Emily nodded placatingly. She hated when Arthur got like this—he was normally such a gentlemen. At first, he'd told her that he only did drugs at parties. Eventually, though, it became clear that he was a fairly regular user. Only recently had he started getting high on their dates, with this time being the worst yet.

Arthur meanwhile dropped his pill onto the dashboard in front of him. "Let's go," he slurred, opening his door.

"You're not seriously going out there, are you?" asked Emily incredulously. "There's no way that they'll let you in like this."

Arthur forcefully grabbed her arm. "We're late to the movie. Late…" He trailed off, momentarily forgetting where he was. "Late!"

"I think we should stay in here for a little bit," Emily said soothingly.

Arthur smiled and shut the door. Without warning, he lunged at Emily, aggressively kissing her neck while clutching her dress.

"Arthur, stop." Her heart began beating faster and faster. "Hey!" It was completely dark around them, with no one in sight. "Arthur!"

"Yeah, babe?" he said, his eyes half shut.

Emily paused. "I have to go and get something."

"Get what?"

She thought quickly. "A…a box."

Arthur pondered this for a moment. "Oh yeah," he said, loosening his grip on Emily. "A box. Well, don't take too long." What was in this mysterious box, he wasn't entirely sure. It certainly seemed important.

"I'll be right back," Emily assured him, slowly sliding out of the car. She gave Arthur a final look and then bolted toward the front of the theater. Flying through the entrance, she hurried over to a crowded area near the concession stand, took out her phone, and desperately dialed her mother.

"Hello?"

"Mom, it's me. I need you to pick me up."

"Emily? Are you okay? Where are you?"

"I'm fine, I'm fine. I'm at the movie theater."

"What happened?"

"Nothing happened. Can you please just come?"

"Of course. I'm on my way."

Emily hung up and put the phone back in her pocket. She walked over to an empty bench behind a poster, watching happy couples holding hands. Tears rolled down her cheeks, the warm water chilled by the icy air of reality. That was the last time she ever talked to Arthur Noir.

* * *

Arthur, who was still quite intoxicated, retrieved his white pill and swallowed it. Growing impatient, he stumbled out of the Porsche, wondering what was so special about a stupid box. It had been a long time since Emily left, and he vaguely remembered being late for something. In a confused panic, Arthur got back into the car, slowly lowering his foot onto the accelerator. He zoomed across the parking lot and onto the street, lights blurring together in amazing patterns. Car horns were honking all around him. They sounded like pineapple, he thought.

Arthur turned onto a dimly lit road, where a shoal of houses lumbered along their concrete foundations—tentacle by tentacle—in the inky blackness. High up in one of them appeared his mother, snorting cocaine and yelling at him before jumping out the window. Arthur closed his eyes, trying to imagine himself walking down a busy street, holding an ice cream cone, somewhere very far away. Back in reality— that tedious place—the Porsche rammed into a stop sign.

"Crash," noted Arthur, to no one in particular. He yanked the steering wheel to the left, smashing into the curb and flattening a mailbox. Taking his foot off the gas pedal, he let the car gradually roll to a stop on someone's front lawn. A few of the houses lit up, and people walked outside.

"Hi," said Arthur, crawling out of the car. He threw up on the door and then collapsed onto the grass. The world around him was getting progressively brighter and louder, causing his head to start throbbing painfully. After two minutes he passed out, his uncle's Porsche dented and covered with vomit, his girlfriend crying and alone, and his life rapidly spiraling into the abyss.

Chapter XXI
Reflection

Much had transpired over the past eighteen months. Though he had only grown a few inches, Christopher looked substantially older, with newly toned muscles complementing stubbly facial hair. His wardrobe had likewise completely changed: collared shirts and colorful sweaters having been replaced by V-necks and leather jackets. Despite the residual awkwardness left over from puberty, Christopher was objectively handsome, although he personally couldn't see it. All he noticed was how closely he resembled his father.

Beyond the physical, Christopher had developed a reputation as somewhat of a tough guy, rarely speaking up in class. He still maintained flawless grades, but he did so covertly and without any obvious effort. Whenever report cards were handed out, he would stare with disappointment at his column of A's, crumple up the paper, and then toss it into the trash can. Semester after semester, his achievements found their way into the school dumpster, balled up brilliance discarded like dreams on a deathbed.

Christopher had gotten his license as soon as he was of age, and now he passed the time driving around, exploring the city as if it were an exotic new world. When he wasn't traveling the streets, he was playing basketball. His hard work was finally paying dividends, both on and off the court. With Jack's departure for college, Christopher became the team's starting point guard, thereby garnering constant female attention. Contrary to popular belief, however, he had yet to kiss a girl.

At home, things were going less smoothly. Arthur had been arrested for his drug-induced escapade, and while he insisted that it was an isolated incident, the costly damage to the Porsche had guaranteed his uncle's outrage. The two of them barely talked to each other these days—divided by an invisible wall that separated their dual realities. For the moment, at least, Christopher was on his father's side. He had been told in vague terms how Arthur had treated Emily, and in spite of his hardened exterior, Christopher still despised injustice.

Furthermore, he cared deeply about Emily, more than she knew. She had replaced Arthur as his closest companion, not by time spent together but by, well, affection, for lack of a better word. She had invited him to her annual New Year's Eve party, and he had accepted without hesitation. Her parents were out of town this weekend, which would surely translate into a night of debauchery and mayhem.

Christopher turned onto the unfamiliar street, slowing down to look for Emily's house. Spotting what looked to be it, he pulled up to the curb, searching for signs of life. Behind him, the road he had taken was not only empty, it looked almost unreal. In front of him, the same street extended out into the unknown, devoid of humanity. Perhaps in that blackness he would find what he was looking for, but at present he was completely alone.

Christopher parked and emerged from the black Ford hatchback that he shared with his cousin. The address on the sidewalk was indeed Emily's, but for some reason there was not a single other car in sight. Christopher felt his heart beating against his chest, like a small child banging on the doors of a grimy dungeon. A single bead of icy sweat trickled down his nose and dropped with a hiss onto the blacktop below. He exhaled nervously, watching his breath turn white in the frigid December air, shivering as the last of his innocence dissipated into obscurity.

In the passenger side window, Christopher made out the shape of a strange figure. It was a boy—a man, really. The man's body was entirely covered by dark clothes, his hair was combed back in dark streaks, and his lips were curved up at the corners into a dark grin. The man in the window was not afraid of some party, or of anything for that matter. On the inside, Christopher was still that green-shoed first grader walking into Mrs. Wright's class. But on the outside, he had unwittingly transformed into this alien being, too slowly to notice yet too quickly to reconsider.

In the muted glow of the streetlights, the man that was his reflection nodded with confidence, and

Christopher nodded back. This was who he was now. This was the man he had become. He looked up the at night sky, making eye contact with the white moon. He was no longer subject to its panoptic supremacy, for at this moment, he was invincible.

Christopher locked his car and approached Emily's home. No lights were on inside, and given the time, he opted not to ring the doorbell. Pacing purposefully across the front lawn, he saw that the gate leading to the backyard was open. Emanating from it came the faint sound of music coupled with laughter, which steadily increased in volume as he neared the house. Taking a deep breath, Christopher walked through the gate and into adulthood.

Chapter XXII
Flare

Christopher transitioned between circles of loose acquaintances, listening to superficial conversations in silence. He had only been to a handful of parties before, and not once had he ever felt comfortable, let alone carefree. For some reason, Christopher almost never found himself at ease with other people, and as a result he chose to adopt personalities better suited to his environment. It was an exhausting lifestyle: having to constantly change costumes for his present company. But what choice did he have? No one would ever understand who he was beneath his disguises, perhaps not even Christopher himself.

A freezing wind rushed by unannounced. Christopher rubbed his hands together inside his jacket pocket, his teeth chattering uncontrollably. The other partygoers seemed not to notice the chill: most of them were already drunk, and almost all of them were giggling with a juvenile euphoria unique to these occasions. Christopher watched a girl stumble across the backyard, clearly inebriated. He himself had never tried alcohol, for lack of opportunity more than anything. Christopher looked around nervously. If ever there was a time to drink, it was right now.

Christopher walked over to a table topped with bottles and cups, pouring himself a large amount of vodka.

"You want some soda?" asked a tall, red-haired kid. He was wearing a frayed hoodie and several thick chains, though despite his somewhat threatening attire, his boyish face gave off the impression that he was completely harmless.

"I already got something, thanks," said Christopher, holding up his cup.

"You're drinking that straight? You might not want to do that."

Christopher shrugged and took what he immediately realized was too large a swig. He spit out repeatedly, his eyes tearing up. "Gross."

The boy laughed. "Try mixing it."

Christopher added in some lemon-lime soda and took a much smaller sip. It was still fairly disgusting, but infinitely more tolerable than the first time.

"That was fantastic," said Christopher pleasantly, his urge to fit in overpowering his truthful disposition. "Thanks for the tip."

"No problem. Is this your first party?"

"Nah, I party a ton. I just don't usually drink."

"Cool, man. My name's Matthew, by the way."

"Nice to meet you. I'm Christopher."

"Hey, did you ever have Mrs. Wright or Mr. Richardson?"

"Yeah, I had both of those teachers." Christopher thought for a second. "Oh, Matthew! I'm sorry, I didn't recognize you. Wow, you've changed a lot." He wasn't picking his nose, for one thing. And he'd roughly doubled in size.

"You've changed too. In a good way, I think. To be honest, most of elementary school is a blur."

"Totally. Well, I'll see you soon, I guess."

Matthew held up a peace sign with one hand and a red plastic cup with the other. "Later, dude."

Christopher watched him disappear into the sea of people, another memory coming and going like the ocean tides. Every year, he had anxiously awaited his birthday, excited to be moving another step closer to maturity and independence. But now that he was almost there, time seemed to be speeding up, and he longed for his childhood. Unlike his next birthday, however, youth would only drift farther and farther away into the deep.

Christopher shook his head: he was thinking too much. He forced himself to down the entire drink in his hand, and then walked over to a newly kindled firepit. The flames danced and crackled, tiny trails of light amidst the oppressive winter darkness.

Christopher huddled close to the fire, soaking in its warmth. He watched the blazing wood turn to ashes, unable to handle the intense heat without disintegrating into slivers of black. The kids sitting next to him were nothing more than extras in this scene: strangers living in a world of strangers. Christopher only really *knew* two people: his father and his cousin. And neither of them knew him, beyond catching infrequent glimpses of his true identity. Perhaps it was Christopher who was the stranger.

"Christopher!"

He turned around, only to be engulfed by Emily's arms. He started to pull back after about a second, but she still clung to him. Finally she let go and they sat down together next to the fire.

"Great party," he said.

"You think so?" she asked shivering. "It's so cold out here."

Christopher removed his jacket and put it over her shoulders. Emily looked up at him flirtatiously.

"I'm going to go get something to drink," she said. "Want anything?"

"No thanks."

Emily returned with a bottle of beer and a gargantuan grin.

"I'm drunk," she stated happily, falling onto Christopher's lap.

"Careful."

"You're such a good friend," she said. "So many guys I've met are just...they just want certain things. All of them are assholes." Her face darkened, burdened by the weight of her past. Suddenly she was back. "Not you, though. You're so nice." She leaned over and hugged him again, laughing nonsensically.

"Are you feeling all right?" he asked.

"Blue eyes," she responded, nearly touching his iris with her finger before kissing his cheek. He pulled away—this was not how he had envisioned the dawn of their romance.

"Let's do some shots," Emily slurred.

"Maybe we should go inside," said Christopher protectively.

Emily smiled and grabbed his hand. The two of them entered the empty house, flipping on the lights. Emily staggered into the kitchen, where she hit her side on the countertop and fell to the floor.

"Emily!"

"I don't feel good," she announced.

Christopher helped her up and guided her to the bathroom.

"Why don't you rest in there," he said. "Take as much time as you need. I'll be out here waiting for you."

Fifteen minutes later, Emily began to sob.

"Is everything fine?" asked Christopher. No reply. "Can I come in?" Still nothing. "Okay, I'm going to walk in now." He opened the door to find Emily huddled up in the bathtub, his jacket wrapped around her like a blanket. He approached her slowly, sat down behind her, and put his hands on her shoulders. "I've got you," he said instinctively. "I've got you."

After some time, Emily turned around. "I'm feeling a lot better now," she said, still crying. "I just felt dizzy, like I was gonna pass out. I'm so sorry about earlier. I didn't mean to make you feel weird."

"You didn't," assured Christopher.

Emily looked at him for ages, her tears falling onto his jacket. "I think I ruined this," she said eventually, pointing to the wet leather.

"I don't mind. What's bothering you?"

"It's a lot of things. I mean, my parents are getting divorced, all the guys I've ever dated are evil—normal stuff, I guess. I just keep trusting people, because what the hell else am I supposed to do? And those people keep letting me down." She paused to wipe her nose. "I'm terrified to let anyone into my life, so I don't. And I know that I can't live like this forever, but I also can't handle being disappointed again. I just feel really alone right now."

"Being smart can get lonely sometimes," said Christopher, almost to himself.

Emily was quiet for a minute before resuming her lament. "I hate thinking about things," she said with troubling composure. "When I get drunk, I don't have to think about anything. It's really freeing, but it's also so scary, having to escape all the time." Her cries became hysterical again. "I don't want to be sober anymore. I don't want to think anymore."

Christopher wreathed his arms around Emily. "Everything is going to be fine," he soothed, suddenly very confident in that statement. Emily smiled spontaneously, her lips parting slightly in the middle. Christopher smiled back as the countdown to the New Year began outside. Ten, nine, eight.

"Looks like we're gonna miss the ball drop," Emily said. Seven, six, five.

"Bummer," said Christopher, his heart pounding faster and faster with every second. Four, three, two.

Emily looked up at him, her eyes reflecting starlight. One.

Christopher kissed Emily. The whole world went white, his soul shining through his body like a solar flare. He'd heard that the first kiss was supposed to be awkward, but nothing he'd ever done had felt so natural. This was the reason for it all. This was his empyreal endeavor.

They kept going for a whole minute. Christopher finally stopped, and Emily rested her head against his neck.

"Happy New Year," he whispered.

Chapter XXIII
Blue

Christopher reclined on the living room couch, watching a TV special about space. Emily's legs rested on a silk pillow to his left, while her pale head leaned against his own. On the screen, the universe was black and abstract. In his heart, Emily was white and tangible, divine even. He watched as her eyelids drifted downward with beautiful slowness, fairylike.

Christopher suddenly pictured his mother, remembered looking into her eyes—now mythic in his mind—as she read to him with her undulating cadence. It was his only vivid memory of her, the final stone remaining from an ancient monument. This was the first time he had heard her voice in years—it sounded disturbingly like Emily's, he thought. Maybe it was merely a memory of a memory; maybe the stone was a fake; maybe the monument never really existed at all.

Emily wasn't nearly as interested in the science show as Christopher, evidenced by the fact that she was now sleeping serenely on his shoulder. Christopher carefully reached for the remote and lowered the volume. Fortunately, he could still hear the dignified

British narrator rambling on about the immensity of everything. As he spoke, innumerable stars illuminated the screen, huge balls of plasma darting across the plasma television.

Christopher looked back at Emily, whose hair twisted around her slightly open mouth and fell onto his shirt. It was hard to believe that only two months had passed since the party. How had he survived beforehand, before her? Since then, everything had been almost too incredible, causing Christopher to worry that his newfound happiness was not a profound and permanent bliss but a trifling and temporary high. In truth, Emily was a drug—intoxicating—and he was most definitely addicted.

On some level, Christopher recognized the total and absolute coldness of the world; he knew that souls and spirits were simply constructs created to conceal the chemical composition of the human brain. But with Emily, he felt warm, burning with fiery purpose. Perhaps it was love, perhaps not. Certainly, though, it was real. His soul, however illusory, fused together atoms of emotion within his astral core.

"Stars are the grand guardians of the galaxy," the narrator poeticized. "They light up the universe and shine on far off worlds."

An enormous blue star came into focus, taking up the entire display. Christopher was transfixed, his blue eyes widening with wonder.

"The largest stars are called hypergiants," continued the narrator. "Exponentially larger than our own sun, hypergiants are powerful beyond compare, ruling unchallenged over their planetary subjects. But like all great monarchs, they cannot reign forever. When one dies, its supernova creates a massive black hole, which then consumes all that is of matter. From the brightest suns arise the darkest voids: infinitely destructive yet fundamentally barren."

* * *

A shiny limousine drifted in front of a menacing alleyway. Apart from two blinking neon signs, the street looked deserted, and the alley itself was pitch-black.

Precisely as the car came to a stop, a large, frightening man crawled out of the backseat, while Arthur reluctantly followed him into the night. Another man, even more intimidating than the first, emerged behind them. He hurriedly opened the passenger door for a suited gentleman with a sharp haircut, whose very presence in this part of town implied that something was seriously amiss.

"Over there," he said, motioning toward a dark corner under an overhang. One of his henchmen walked Arthur to the spot, and then removed his jacket to reveal a fairly sizable handgun. The gentleman—accompanied by his other bodyguard—strolled over to meet them, making eye contact with Arthur the entire time.

"Do you know who I am?" he asked.

"No," replied Arthur honestly, trying to mask his apprehension.

"My name is Mr. Gates, but all you need to know is that I'm someone who you shouldn't make angry."

"I can see that, sir."

"Well, it seems you did so anyway. You know that stuff you sold to Frankie last week? That stuff was no good."

"You work with Frankie?" asked Arthur.

Mr. Gates laughed derisively. "Frankie works for me," he said. "Actually, Frankie works for another guy, who works for another guy, who works for me. And you sold him garbage."

"I'm sorry," said Arthur. "I've never had problems with my stuff before."

"Yeah, well now you do. You owe me six hundred. Get it by next Friday and give it to Frankie at your usual place, or we'll have a much less friendly discussion."

"My usual place?"

"Don't think for a second that I don't know about you, kid. You're not the worst dealer I've seen, but you've got a lot to learn. Let's just hope I don't need to give you any more lessons." Mr. Gates walked back to the limo and hopped inside. Arthur began to head over, but the larger bodyguard stopped him.

"We're done here," he said.

"But I have to get back," Arthur pleaded. "I have no idea where we are, and I got no money for a cab. What am I supposed to do?"

"Enjoy the scenery," the thug suggested, before walking away. The car silently zoomed off, leaving Arthur by himself in the slum. He fished through his pocket and pulled out five pills: two red, two gray, and one that was nearly as blue as he was. No longer concerned about his own mortality, Arthur swallowed them all and retreated back into the darkness.

After some time, a deranged tramp stumbled toward him from across the street. He was singing, in the absolute loosest sense of the word, while swaying wildly from side to side. Arthur didn't bother to flee; he probably looked just as insane himself.

"I hear babies cry," the lunatic rasped, "I watch them grow."

Arthur's world started to fade as the pills took effect.

"They'll learn much more," groaned the maniac, coughing repeatedly, "than I'll ever know."

Arthur slapped himself under the waxing moon to rouse his waning consciousness.

"And I think to myself..."

Arthur's eyes closed, his arms extended out onto the dirty pavement, and his head landed with a thud onto the building behind him.

"What a wonderful world."

Chapter XXIV
Beauty

Christopher knelt down on the graveyard grass, watching a ladybug ascend a tall dandelion. So delicately it climbed that the thin stem did not bend or pitch beneath its weight, so slowly it moved that after several minutes it was still inches from the flower. Just then, the gentlest of zephyrs swept in from the opposite side, scattering hundreds of florets into the sky while surely striking mortal terror into the heart of the ladybug. This soft breeze on Christopher's skin was a sudden catastrophe for the cemetery creatures; indeed, a mere footstep could lay waste to an entire insect metropolis.

From Christopher's lofty stance, the plight of the ladybug was admittedly unmoving. On this field alone, billions of bees, beetles, and butterflies buzzed and bumbled around in the grass, desperately searching for food and mates purely out of instinct. Granted, these beings were alive just like Christopher; they were made of the same basic elements as he was. But it was nevertheless apparent that their brief stay on earth was utterly inconsequential, that their actions and attitudes had no grand implications or moral underpinnings. Should the ladybug go on to thrive and enjoy bountiful aphids for the remainder of its life, or should it die a gruesome death within the hour, the universe would continue on unchanged. Either outcome would be just another thing that happened, or didn't happen.

* * *

Christopher approached his mother's headstone with slow, deferential strides. He hadn't been here in many years—too many years. At first, he had avoided coming back to the church and its graveyard out of pain: both places were fraught with unpleasant remembrances. After a couple years, not visiting his mother became almost customary, unquestioned. And recently, if he was being honest with himself, he had simply forgotten about her. The dead have a strange way of not attracting attention.

Sitting down in front of the stone, Christopher ran his finger along the words engraved in the white marble. Something about his mother's maiden name, which she had made her middle name upon marriage, resonated with him: Blanche. He again traced out the letters, felt their permanence on his fingertip. All at once, Christopher recognized that underneath him rested an actual person. She was real—not a memory of a memory but someone he had loved. Suddenly he was cold; shivers chilled his spine and brought him to tears. He embraced the tombstone, completely overwhelmed, wet drops falling like rain onto the dry, inanimate rock.

In the distance, the church bell began to ring. Christopher—a new man—looked up at the steeple where the bell tolled. Above it, the old cross watched over him as it always had, while his own cross hung down below his neck, neglected but still there, shining with the light of bygone faith.

Intellectually, Christopher knew that he and the ladybug were more or less the same, operating entirely on impulse. Yet the way he felt about his mother had to be more than chemical attachment, and his affection for Emily clearly surpassed the realm of science. These emotions demanded spiritual meaning, his actions required ethical polarity, or else nothing would any make sense.

Then and there, alone with the faithful dead, Christopher had his penultimate epiphany. God came to him—well, really, he came to God—and his world went white. The wind that threatened the ladybug would no longer blow him off course; the tides of inevitability could not pull him adrift. He had risen above the random unfeelingness of reality and joined its transcendent counterpart, where the world shimmered with blinding beauty. Once again, everything would matter, his life would be significant, if only in his mind.

* * *

A week after Christopher went to the graveyard, Anthony handed him his Saturday morning list of chores—which as usual he had scrawled onto a sheet of notepaper—before going to play golf with some of his new cultured friends. Christopher watched him leave, scanned the mundane tasks, and then peered out a window at the mountains that towered above his city. He felt a sudden desire to scale those peaks, to escape his trivial existence for as long as possible. He wanted to look down upon the earth from a height sufficient to observe divine planning, or at least from high enough to pretend.

In an unprecedented and glorious moment of spontaneity, Christopher discarded the list and drove toward Emily's house. After convincing her to accompany him on his quest, they headed straight for the hills, where they spent the day climbing a steep trail. At present, Emily was exhausted, willing herself over the final stone step of a switchback before collapsing onto the chalky mountainside.

"I...I can't...I need to stop," she panted.

"Don't worry about it," said Christopher, wiping the sweat off his brow while handing Emily his water jug. She gratefully accepted it—her bottle, like her energy reserves, had been largely depleted for much of the hike. Taking a lengthy sip, she wriggled back onto a flat, prismatic boulder that resembled a Grecian plinth. Fitness was hardly a pillar of her character, though never before had her poor stamina been so remorselessly exposed.

"You probably hate me for making you do this," said Christopher, sitting down next to Emily.

"No, I'm glad I came. I obviously needed the exercise."

"You did great," he praised.

"Thanks, but you don't have to say that. I know my limitations." Emily laughed. "You can keep going, Christopher. I don't want to hold you back."

Christopher didn't reply. Instead, he rotated around to face the distant summit: that place universally accepted as the ultimate goal. Emily was not capable of reaching it, while Christopher was satisfied to stand atop this lower plateau. Ultimately, their paths intertwined—they were both trekking uphill against the natural gradient, jointly lost on the journey to some predetermined point. Perhaps they were merely ladybugs.

Meanwhile, Christopher's silence was making Emily feel guilty. "I'm sorry," she said, having caught her breath. "This must be awful for you."

Christopher scooted closer to her. "Awful," he repeated playfully.

Emily smiled and began fiddling with his cross necklace. From their elevated perch, the pair surveyed the vast expanse below them. Majestic pines and crystal lakes stretched out absurdly in every direction, forcing Christopher to question the veracity of his world.

"Beautiful," said Emily eventually. Christopher turned toward her.

"Beautiful," he echoed, admiring the whites of her ethereal eyes. Then they kissed for a long time, separated from reality by a mutual denial of its truths, held together by the shared sensation of something greater than those truths could explain. Christopher wasn't sure how long he could maintain that separation;

he couldn't tell if Emily was that something greater. But for now, it didn't matter.

"Before I got to know you, I was so confused," Emily reflected. "I always felt like I was part of this incredible thing, but it wasn't until we started dating that I really understood it. We're all pieces of it—this beauty." She looked almost angelic, her words flowing in harmony with the waterfall to her right. "It's like God is showing me my destiny. You know what I mean?"

"I love you," Christopher said for the first time, without fully considering the gravity of his words. He was certainly experiencing a powerful new emotion, and he might as well call it love.

Emily looked at him: her savior, her purpose. "I love you too," she said confidently, pulling him closer with his cross.

Chapter XXV
Gun

Arthur knocked twice on the bronze oak. Ten seconds later, a tall, red-haired boy peered through the peephole and then opened the door.

"Hey, how are you?" Arthur asked, solely due to convention.

"I've been better," replied Matthew. Lines of fatigue were etched beneath his eyes, which along with his condiment-stained sweatpants made him look less than professional. Still, Arthur knew he could be trusted.

"You can come in," he said eventually. "Nobody's here except us." Arthur followed him through the apartment, noticing the general disarray of its fixtures and fittings.

"Nice place," Arthur commented facetiously.

"It is what it is," said Matthew, without breaking stride. "I'm planning to move out after I graduate."

"Me too, man. I can't wait to get away from my goddamn family."

"Oh, speaking of which, I saw Christopher at a party a few months ago. How's he doing? You know we went to the same elementary school, right?"

"I didn't know that," said Arthur. "I honestly don't know how he is; we don't talk that much anymore. I mean, he *seems* all right. He's got a girlfriend now, if you can believe that."

"Is she hot?"

"Yeah, I think so. I dated her for a bit, but she's really straitlaced—like Christopher." He glanced at the ceiling, either distracted or distressed.

"You know what's funny? The two of you aren't all that different on the inside. It's almost like you really are brothers."

Arthur laughed dismissively and walked with Matthew into the kitchen—or at least the area with kitchen appliances. Actually cooking there would be a threat to public health.

"You can sit down if you want," said Matthew, motioning toward his dining room table. "I'll be right back." He receded into a dark hallway, emerging after a minute with a brown paper bag. Arthur grabbed it and removed a black, unbranded, semi-automatic pistol.

"There are about thirty rounds in there. Hopefully you won't need more than that."

"It's just for protection," said Arthur, inspecting the gun excitedly. "I had a run-in with a dissatisfied customer—guy named Mr. Gates."

"Is he after you?"

"Nah, all he wants is cash, which I've got."

"Still better to be prepared."

"Exactly. I assume this thing is clean?"

"Of course, man. It's totally off the radar—no ID or anything."

"So how much is this gonna cost me?"

"Consider it a gift. It sounds like you'll need it."

"You sure?"

"What goes around comes around," said Matthew, oddly cheerful. "Karma, dude."

"Well, all right. I appreciate the help." Arthur got up and walked toward the exit, tucking the pistol under his belt. It looked natural there, fated. He opened the door, a legitimate gangster.

"Good luck," chirped Matthew.

Arthur smiled. "I got all the luck I need right here, thanks to you," he said, pointing to the gun and then closing the door behind him.

* * *

Christopher read the final lines of *The Stranger* with mild frustration. He'd been looking for his Bible, which was accumulating dust beneath Camus's masterpiece, when he decided to finally finish Arthur's favorite book.

"I laid my heart open to the benign indifference of the universe," said Meursault, the protagonist, the stranger. A troubling sentiment, thought Christopher. Something Arthur would say. He picked up the novel and walked into the hall. Upon reaching Arthur's room, he turned the door handle, but it was locked.

"Who is it?" Arthur called out.

"It's me," said Christopher, surprised that Arthur was home for once.

"Give me a second," he said. Arthur quickly closed a box and shoved it under his bed. It was hardly a safe hiding place, but for the moment it would suffice.

"What are you doing in there?" asked Christopher.

"Nothing," Arthur said, finally opening the door. "What's up?"

"I just wanted to give this back to you," said Christopher, handing Arthur the book. "Thanks again for letting me read it."

"No problem," he said. "What did you think?"

"It was all right."

"Just all right?"

"I mean, it was interesting, but I couldn't relate to Meursault. He kills that one guy for basically no reason."

"That's kind of the point, though, isn't it? We make life out to be so special and holy, but really it's all nonsense."

"I found God," said Christopher suddenly.

"When?" asked Arthur.

"Yesterday."

"Do you feel happier?"

"Yeah, I think. It's reassuring, knowing that your life means something."

"Cool," said Arthur, with barefaced disdain.

Christopher scratched his head awkwardly. "Okay, well, I'll see you later," he said, starting to leave.

Upon reaching the door, he had a thought and turned around. "Hey, what was it that you were doing before?"

Arthur forced himself to look away from the bed and toward his desk. "Organizing," he said, not altogether dishonestly.

"For what?"

"Don't worry about it."

"Whatever," said Christopher, accustomed to Arthur's mysterious nature. "Oh, I don't know if you heard, but I have a playoff game tomorrow afternoon. I know that it's Friday and you probably have plans, but the game's right after school, if you want to come."

"Sorry, man, I got some stuff I need to take care of tomorrow. Good luck, though."

"Thanks. If you change your mind, get there early. It should be packed."

"I will. How is school, by the way?"

"It's fine. You should show up sometime." Christopher laughed and left the room.

Arthur watched him go and then retrieved the box. He had eight hundred seventeen dollars in there—more than enough to repay Frankie. Everything was going to be fine, he told himself. He removed the pistol, concealing it under his jacket. A little insurance couldn't hurt.

* * *

The next morning, Anthony awoke gasping for breath, asphyxiated by his own mucus. He cleared his raw throat several times and then checked the clock, which displayed 5:47 in shining blood-red. Just looking at the light proved brutally unpleasant, so he covered his eyes with a blanket and curled up into a ball of misery.

After forty-five minutes, Anthony finally fell back asleep, at which time his alarm mercilessly sounded. He listened in agony to it beeping—becoming incrementally louder each time—unable to summon the energy to turn it off. A sudden bolt of lightning stabbed through the sky outside his bedroom window, simultaneously epitomizing and exacerbating his headache. He slammed off the alarm and rolled over, sweating profusely whilst deathly cold. This was clearly not his day.

Shortly thereafter, Christopher hurried into the room. "Dad, wake up. It's time to go." Anthony didn't respond. "Dad!"

"Huh? What?"

"We have to leave. Right now."

"I'm feeling awful, buddy. Can you and Arthur ride together?"

"Arthur isn't here, Dad. He left with the Ford."

"Perfect," Anthony said bitterly. "Well, I suppose you can take my car."

"Thanks, Dad. Feel better."

Anthony watched him go, grateful that he still had one responsible child. Arthur was a different story. Where on earth did he spend his time? He was never at school or at home, and he didn't have many friends. Gathering his limited strength, Anthony lifted himself out of bed and stumbled into Arthur's room. He was going to solve this mystery, whatever that entailed.

Anthony carefully searched through the closet and the drawers, making sure to return everything to its previous place. So far, leaving aside the horrendous smell and the general chaos, nothing in the room was even remotely suspect. Out of ideas and thoroughly tired, Anthony was about to go back to sleep when he saw something protruding out slightly from under Arthur's bed. Kneeling down beside it, he pulled out an unmarked black box, which had only been placed there by pure happenstance. Much of life—and death—is brutally random.

Debating whether he wanted to know the box's contents, Anthony sat thinking for several minutes. Finally, he removed the lid. Every kind of drug imaginable, along with some that were unimaginable, lay tightly packed inside. Anthony, still in shock, rummaged through the contraband. Dozens of tens and twenties padded the bottom of the box, perhaps a thousand dollars in cash. Anthony looked away in disgust: Arthur was a drug dealer.

Chapter XXVI
Love

Christopher fiercely flung elbows left and right, then soared for the rebound. He clutched the ball with both hands, screaming, having morphed into a rabid beast in order to contend with his larger adversaries. But the beast was running on fumes, and after four quarters and two overtime periods, he and the other players were battling simply to stand upright.

"Timeout!" yelled Coach Johnson, running onto the court to make himself audible over the raucous crowd. "Timeout!!!"

The referee finally heard him and blew the whistle. Christopher slowly wobbled to the bench, leaning over to hear his coach detail a play. It was a good thing he was so fatigued: he lacked the energy to be nervous.

"Four seconds left, boys," Coach hollered above the roar of the arena. "They're only up by one. If we score, we win and advance to the city championship. This is it. You've lived your life for this moment." The players nodded in unison.

"So what's the play, Coach?" panted one of them.

"Andrew, you stand here and screen for Jason. He'll be a decoy. Christopher, you're gonna take the shot to win this ballgame for us."

"Me?" Christopher asked.

"You've been our point guard and our leader all year long. You've worked the hardest. You've made the right decisions. You're the smartest player I've ever coached. And I trust you." He looked at Christopher, whose sweating face oozed determination. "Are you ready to be a star?"

"Yes, sir."

"All right, then. Win on three. One, two, three..."

"Win!!!" the team shouted together.

Christopher walked back onto the court, sneaking a glance at his father. Despite his deathly sickness and his sickening discovery, Anthony had been cheering Christopher throughout. Now he smiled weakly from the crowd, nearly as exhausted as the players. It was just like their backyard showdown of three years prior, with Christopher preparing for the final shot and Anthony trying not to throw up.

Jason inbounded the ball to Christopher and then ran to the three-point line. Andrew—either mesmerized by the situation or about to pass out—failed to set the screen. But it didn't matter. There was only Christopher and the basket, the world beyond the hardwood blurred, and everything went silent. He dribbled to the foul line, grabbed the ball, jumped with every ounce of power in his muscles, and only when he reached the apex of his leap did he look up. The clock above the backboard ticked down to one second. His defender was too low to block his shot. Christopher released the ball with perfect spin and perfect focus, and it swished through the net precisely as the buzzer sounded.

Christopher closed his eyes. All around him, his triumphant teammates held up their hands and pumped their fists, while his opponents cried and hustled to their locker room. Christopher felt strangely numb, his mind already occupied by other thoughts, the moment having come and gone like any other.

Christopher, underneath his joyful expression, was deeply pensive during the car ride home, with Coach Johnson's speech echoing continuously in his head: "This is it. You've lived your life for this moment." Was that shot really the zenith of his existence? Sure, he was happy. But like his time with Emily, his present exuberance felt like a drug-induced high—fleeting and insubstantial.

Anthony's mind was necessarily fixed on Arthur. Had he been too lenient with the boy, allowing him to get away with more and more until he became a criminal? Or had he acted too harshly, compelling Arthur to rebel against his oppressive authority? Either way, Anthony realized, it was certainly his fault. Pulling into the garage, he sighed with regret, having failed his adopted son. All the while, a single black crow rested atop the Wilsons' mailbox, waiting.

* * *

Arthur tore down the very foundations of the house, emptying every cabinet and cupboard. He'd had enough of disappearing boxes for one lifetime: the first had cost him his girlfriend; the second might cost him his life.

"Where is it?" he cried. "Where is it?" He was supposed to meet Frankie that night, and showing up without the money was simply not an option. To make matters worse, the meth that he'd smoked earlier was making him extremely paranoid, a feeling that at present seemed highly reasonable. After an hour of fruitlessly searching for his drug money, Arthur retired to the sofa, taking out his pistol.

"Anthony," he whispered through clenched teeth. "Give me back my box."

* * *

Anthony entered the kitchen—its floor hardly visible beneath jagged piles of forks, knives, and plates—stunned by the surely burglarized state of his longtime home. He dialed the police, directing Christopher to go into his room and lock the door. Meanwhile, Arthur, who had fallen into somewhat of a trance, awakened and rose to his feet.

"Where's the box?" he asked, holding back inhuman rage. His eyes shone red, his body shook, and his right index finger rested dangerously close to the trigger of his gun.

Anthony froze, dropping the phone. "Arthur, calm down," he managed eventually.

"Where's...the...box?"

"What? What box?"

"You know exactly what goddamn box!!!"

"It's all right," said Anthony peaceably. "I'm gonna go get the box now. Just put the gun down, and I'll give it to you."

Arthur was not about to fall for this trick again. "Stay where you are!" he commanded. "Tell me where it is!"

"I'm just going into my bedroom to get your box. I'll walk slowly. You can follow me if you want."

"I already checked your bedroom! It's not there!"

"It's in the safe. I'll go get it. Please, Arthur, put down the gun."

"9-1-1, what is your emergency?" came a faint voice. The phone sat on a large assemblage of broken glass, apparently still in working order.

"You called the cops on me?" asked Arthur, incredulous.

"No," said Anthony, panicking. "I thought we'd been robbed." He scrambled to the ground and hung up the phone. "Everything's okay now."

"You called the cops," repeated the drugged Arthur, clearly removed from reality. He pointed his pistol squarely at Anthony's chest. "You took my box and then tried to get me arrested."

"Please," begged Anthony. "Please."

Christopher popped up from behind the counter. "Stop it!" he cried.

"It ends here," said Arthur, red eyes locked on his target, hand pressed firmly on the grip of the gun, finger ready to fire.

"I love you, Arthur," said Anthony, just before a bullet pierced his lung. He screamed. Christopher screamed. Arthur fled, and it was over.

Chapter XXVII
Why

Sirens sounded outside in the dying twilight. Police officers broke down the front door and rushed into the house, holding handguns from empty holsters, porcelain plates cracking beneath their boots. Christopher watched them enter peripherally, unable to make out their faces in the shadows of his fading world. His father looked up at him amidst the maelstrom.

"This is definitely not my day," Anthony said softly, his sense of humor fairing far better than his physical form, which clung to life as hopelessly as the sky grasping for the sun at dusk.

"You're gonna get through this, Dad," promised Christopher. He wiped his eyes, his wails belying his projected confidence. Promises, regrettably, were nothing more than words—incapable of resurrecting his mother, powerless to heal his father. Meanwhile, the pool of blood spurting from Anthony's wound continued to grow, flowing past his shirt and staining the base of his neck. Like Christopher, he was only vaguely cognizant of the police presence around him.

"Don't tell them..." Anthony murmured, his susurrations trailing off with his vitality. He paused, gasping for breath. "...that it was Arthur."

"But Dad, he shot you!" cried Christopher. His tears poured onto the ground and coalesced with his father's blood. "He killed you."

"It doesn't matter," said Anthony, almost silently. His eyes went dim, the sun dipped below the horizon, and light became dark.

"Hey, kid, you okay?" asked one of the officers. Christopher knelt beside his father, paralyzed. "Can you hear me?" Silence, no reply, words useless.

A paramedic checked Anthony's pulse as blood seeped from his open mouth. He waited several seconds, then turned to the officer and shook his head. The policeman looked back at Christopher, who had collapsed onto the floor, and cursed his luck. He was going to be so late for dinner.

* * *

Hardly by choice had Christopher returned to the train station. He began walking forward, dazed and disoriented, scanning his surroundings for lurking peddlers. However, unlike the nightmarish pandemonium of his first time here, the building was deserted, and Christopher continued on alone. He wasn't sure which was more unbearable: the suffocating confusion of a thousand vendors attempting to sell him their wares, or the lonesome absence of that confusion altogether. Mrs. Wright, Father Goodson, Jesus—all the salesmen who before had desperately solicited his attention—had vanished from view, their philosophical goods exposed by his disillusionment.

Above him, the sky flashed orange and purple, just as it had more than a decade ago. Suddenly, a proper ceiling began to form, a stone roof covering up the mysteries and uncertainties that lay beyond. Soon the station was fully enclosed, while Christopher aimlessly wandered through the cavernous concourse. The word "why" was scribbled manually onto the wall, its letters spaced out as if written by a child. "W-h-y."

Off in the distance, Christopher spotted a train that had pulled to a stop. He approached it warily, expecting it to disappear as he got closer. But the train stayed put, and in an open railcar stood his father, just where his mother had once been. Christopher ran toward him, and to his surprise he quickly found himself sitting beside the deceased.

The door to the railcar closed, the engine roared into action, and the train slowly edged forward. With unalloyed delight, Christopher looked at his father, whose smile had fossilized onto his rigid face. Something about his expression struck Christopher as mildly terrifying. Turning away, he glanced through a small window in front of him, noticing that the tracks led directly into a black void. Below him, the wheels revolved faster and faster—the train bulleted across the massive station—and with considerable alarm Christopher realized that there was no escape. Father and now son were stuck on their mutual path, the world of potential beyond it was closed off to them permanently, and death was the only way out.

The train picked up speed until it moved irreversibly quickly toward the abyss. Anthony watched unafraid, having resigned himself to his unfortunate fate. Christopher meanwhile frantically fingered for some sort of brake, though at this point nothing could prevent his demise. Utterly trapped, he sat down and calmly awaited the end, his fear quelled by his sorrow. The train shot into the blackness, and Christopher awoke from the dream, but not from the void.

* * *

Christopher stared up at the bright lights of the hospital room, gradually rejoining reality. Feeling a sharp pain from his leg, he checked it, and sure enough it was thoroughly bandaged. As he would later discover, he had injured it fainting onto a bed of silverware. Christopher turned his head to the side, where in the mirror he saw the scar from his previous stay at the hospital. At least this time, unlike with his mother, there was no suspense: he already knew his father was dead.

A nurse came in. "Oh, you're awake," she said passively. "Can I do anything for you?"

Christopher took quite a while to process this question. He eventually asked for some food: he wasn't exactly hungry, but he hadn't eaten in ages. The nurse nodded and exited the room, yawning. It was five o'clock in the morning, the end of her shift, and like the police officer from before she was eager to get home.

Christopher reflected on the absurdity of his present condition. For everyone else, today was a day like any other; for him, today was his first day alone. No longer did he have parents; no longer was he their shining son.

Chapter XXVIII
Supernova

Even the garden-variety supernova is quite rare. Stars can live for billions of years—some nearly date back to the inception of the universe—and each star only dies once, detonates for little more than a minute and is gone forever. A minute out of eternity: a fraction of time mathematically equivalent to zero.

But every so often, an even more extraordinary event unfolds. The singular Type Ia supernova, which can only occur in binary star systems, is a spectacle unmatched by any other. A hypergiant, having already transformed into a white dwarf, sucks up gas from its companion star until it reaches a critical mass. It then explodes with inconceivable power, nay beyond inconceivable, infinite, lighting up the edges of existence. Its mate, the beleaguered second star, the jilted lover, is ejected into the abyss, destined to die alone, the star with which it traveled through the wonders of reality glowing no more.

Emily buried her head in Christopher's black coat, weeping onto his tie as he wrapped his arms around her shoulders. Anthony's funeral was her first glimpse of death, and at the moment she felt as though it had been her own father who had passed away. She simply couldn't bear the idea that something so essential, so integral to one's life could suddenly cease to exist.

Christopher watched the service with an almost tranquil detachment, having run out of tears long ago. After an indeterminate amount of time, Father Goodson, whose presence in Christopher's life had ironically become synonymous with hellish tidings, concluded his cursory remarks.

"Anthony Wilson was a good, godly man," recited the priest, glossing over the legacy of the departed with broad, practiced strokes. "He's smiling down from heaven at this very instant," he continued, while at the same time Anthony was lowered into the ground, lifeless, certain to remain as such forevermore. "Would his son like to say a few words?"

* * *

Christopher stood before the fairly large crowd of teachers and classmates, who all stared at him expectantly. He gazed at the cross atop the steeple, searching for inspiration.

"The first time I came to this church," said Christopher finally, "I was six years old. Back then, I didn't know anything about Jesus or religion or life. It was nice, being clueless. My dad hadn't wanted me to come here. He never really bought into the whole God thing." Christopher looked directly at Father Goodson.

"But yes, he was a good man; a great man." Anthony's former friends and coworkers nodded their agreement.

"My mom, on the other hand, was very religious. It was her faith that defined who she was, and all she wanted was for me to go to church and share that faith with her. My dad loved my mom—I think that's what defined him—and so he conceded. As a family, we went to the cathedral, a day I'll never forget. I was about to walk inside when my mom stopped me and gave me this." Christopher removed his cross necklace and held it up to his face. "She told me that Jesus would protect me, that he loved me. That was the last day I ever saw her." Several people began to sob.

In his mind, Christopher heard his mother scream her final words: "It doesn't matter!" Suddenly, he realized that his father had said exactly the same thing before his death. All at once, everything made sense, or rather, nothing made sense, but the fact that nothing made sense became abundantly clear. Facing the headstones of his parents, Christopher had his greatest epiphany, for lack of a better term.

"It doesn't matter," he said. "Nothing matters." Father Goodson coughed uncomfortably. "My mom was good, and she died. My dad was good, and he died. I keep asking myself why. Why them? Why me? But I get it now: people live, people die, and nothing really changes. Why? Because none of us *matter*." Christopher looked up, feeling the silence.

"The more I live through, the more I understand that everything is completely random. There's no meaning, no logic...no God." Christopher paused, having shocked even himself. "And if there is a God, he obviously couldn't care less about us."

Christopher breathed out, turned around, and stormed off. Emily chased after him, but he ignored her and proceeded farther into the desolate field. Wind rushed in from behind him, and into the breeze he cast his puerile cross. In the graveyard it would remain for eternity, along with countless other misplaced convictions. He felt his body explode in a solar inferno, his innocent past beaming out from his eyes and lighting up the edges of existence. After little more than a minute, the star that was Christopher Wilson glowed no more.

Chapter XXIX
Antidote

Christopher's late grandparents had raised not one but two boys. The second, Anthony, had been somewhat of an afterthought, while conversely William, the first, had borne the crushing weight of his parents' hand-me-down dreams since his conception. William Wilson was a grand name indeed, though it proved less than prophetic. Half a century later, Mr. Wilson, now employed by the local landfill, was known exclusively as Billy.

Billy was ordinary to an extraordinary degree. He was neither tall nor short, fat nor slender, attractive nor unattractive, old nor young, rich nor poor. He had brown hair and brown eyes and a brown house. On weekdays, Billy would wake up every morning at seven, make himself black coffee and buttered toast, drive twenty minutes to the landfill, push and pull the same three levers till sunset, get pizza with his buddies, drive back home, get drunk, and nod off. On Saturdays, he played softball, bought groceries, and did a load of laundry. On Sundays, he went to church—out of habit more than genuine faith—and then saw an action movie. So he lived, week after week, month after month, year after year.

Nothing forced Billy to exist the way he did: forgoing grandeur and ambition for monotony and routine. He was simply content, more so than he would have been as a politician or a doctor, at least. In his youth he'd had several girlfriends, though he never married. And honestly, he was happier by himself. Billy Wilson answered to no man, changed himself for no woman, and that was just the way he liked it.

* * *

Christopher sat across the table from his uncle, who reclined behind a bevy of empty bottles.

"Everything sucks," said Christopher, attempting to elicit a response.

"I guess." Uncle Billy shrugged and took a large swig of beer. Christopher smiled: here, for once, was an adult who didn't pretend to have all the answers.

"Uncle Billy, I'm sorry I haven't asked you this before, but what exactly do you do?"

"No worries, kid. I work at the landfill over by Lake Washington. It ain't glamorous, but it pays the bills. You'd be surprised at the things people throw away; some of our trash used to be pretty amazing. Makes me think about the past, about what could've been." Billy stared introspectively at his drink, then chuckled for no apparent reason.

"What is it?" asked Christopher.

"Nothing. You want some beer?"

"I can't. I'm still in high school."

"In that case, you probably need some." Billy handed Christopher a bottle, and the two of them drank together, not uncle and nephew but man and fellow man. "So, you're supposed to come live with me, if it's cool with you," said Billy casually.

Christopher was surprised, but somehow unmoved. He remembered Arthur's reaction to being told that he was moving to Seattle, suddenly understanding his cousin's indifference. Once you lose your home and your family, even important things seem inconsequential. Christopher sighed heavily: he loathed Arthur with every fiber of his being.

"Well?" asked Billy.

"Sure," Christopher consented.

"It's settled, then. You can sleep in the guest room. I think you're my first guest."

"I'm honored," said Christopher sarcastically.

Billy laughed again, much more enthusiastically than the situation merited. He tipped back his chair, which then tumbled to the floor. "Oh man," he groaned. "I think I've had one too many."

"Maybe you should stop," Christopher suggested.

"It's okay. I get wasted every night, and the next day I'm totally fine."

Christopher suddenly felt a morsel of concern for his uncle, cringing as compassion crawled up his spine like a parasite.

"Just be careful," he said. "My brother—my former cousin—got addicted to drugs. He's not doing very well right now."

"Everyone's addicted to something," Billy said offhandedly. "Success and power, drugs and alcohol, religion and relationships—they're all the same. Whether you're making money or building an empire, getting high or feeling drunk, finding God or falling in love, all you're really doing is taking an antidote."

"An antidote for what?" asked Christopher.

Billy thought for a moment. "Life," he said eventually. Christopher sighed, sincerely hoping that Emily was not merely his addiction. Billy meanwhile began chuckling again, having drained his daily well of wisdom. "Hey," he said loudly, "can I call you Chris? Christopher is so goddamn long."

"Yeah, all right," said Christopher confidently. At that instant, he decided he was sick of his name: it was childish, religious, and admittedly a mouthful. "I actually prefer Chris."

"Cool," Billy said. "Well, looks like it's you and me against the world."

"Against the world," repeated Chris.

Chapter XXX
Kids

Arthur sat shivering outside a derelict diner, breathing hot air onto his icy fingers. He'd been surviving—in a very literal sense—on the one hundred sixty-three dollars he had recovered from his wallet and his former home on the day he shot Anthony. Two weeks later, he was broke, having exhausted his limited funds buying a mixture of cheap nutriment and costly narcotics. With matted hair, bloodshot eyes, and tattered clothes, Arthur appeared more animal than adolescent, while his noisome stench of bodily fluids helped dehumanize him further. He couldn't go anywhere or do anything, both because he was surely wanted by the police—not to mention Mr. Gates—and because, quite frankly, he looked prohibitively disgusting.

But inside his threadbare coat rested a final chance at life, ironically in the form of the same pistol he had used to end the life of someone else. From his vantage point at the very bottom of the world, Arthur stared across the road at a rundown gas station, formulating his desperate yet feasible plan. With nothing left to lose, he began walking purposefully away from the clouded sun and toward his equally nebulous future. The road ahead would not be without its perils, and he couldn't traverse it alone. But although few potential partners would be willing to overlook his bedraggled condition, he believed he was heading in the direction of one of them.

It took Arthur several hours to reach his destination, by which point the day was all but spent. Panting wearily, he knocked twice on the bronze oak, feeling a profound sense of déjà vu. The wood and the handle were exactly the same as before; indeed, the only thing different this time was Arthur himself.

"Who is it?"

"It's Arthur."

"Hey," said Matthew, opening the door. "Where the hell have you—Jesus, what happened?"

"Can I come inside?" asked Arthur faintly.

"Of course."

Arthur entered the apartment. "Are we alone?"

"Yeah, my dad's never around anymore. Are you all right, man? You look like a bum. And you smell like one too."

"Can I use your shower?"

"Um, sure. That's a good idea, actually." Matthew stepped aside as Arthur turned toward the hallway. "Feel free to use my soap and stuff. Just throw away whatever you touch."

"Thank you," said Arthur, coughing. He got into the shower and stayed there for a long while, forcefully scrubbing away layers of cemented filth from his flaking flesh. Expending three razorblades, he shaved not just his beard but also his entire head, chest, and back. When he emerged from the bathroom, he was unrecognizable, having transformed into a hairless shade. So indistinct was he that he very nearly wasn't there, for beneath the scoured grime only a wisp of his true self remained.

"Wow, you cleaned up!" remarked Matthew.

"Can I borrow some clothes?" asked Arthur, covered only by a towel.

"Definitely. You know where I sleep."

Arthur walked into Matthew's room and found his closet. He picked out a fresh pair of underwear, a tee shirt, jeans, socks, an old pair of sneakers, and a black sweatshirt. Putting on the hood, Arthur admired himself in the mirror. He could have been anyone, which was perfect. He slid the barrel of his gun into a pocket, and then paced confidently to the kitchen area.

Matthew inspected his friend. "Looks like you're back, man."

"Let's work together," Arthur said bluntly, his powerful voice having returned along with his dignity.

"Okay," said Matthew, a follower if ever there was one.

"Good." Arthur nodded. "So here's the plan."

* * *

Matthew slowly edged his car into the gas station, stopping at the pump closest to the convenience store. He handed Arthur his joint, figuring that his partner needed another hit. Arthur blew out smoke rings and then hopped out into the cold.

"Wait with the engine on," Arthur said softly, not about to leave his fate up to Matthew's common sense.

"Right," said Matthew, as Arthur closed his door. "I'll be here when you're done."

Arthur's high kicked in at the optimal instant, and with only subliminal dread did he enter the illuminated store, not unlike a mosquito flying toward a bug zapper. Stumbling to the counter, he pulled out his gun.

"Don't move!" he shouted.

"Ah!" exclaimed the clerk, rather predictably. He was young—more boy than man—and he clearly didn't have much experience being robbed.

"Shut up!" said Arthur. "Put all the money in a bag and nobody gets hurt." That sounded credible, he thought.

"Okay, okay." The kid opened up the register and cautiously began removing its contents.

"Faster! Let's go!" The bag quickly filled with cash, mostly small denominations. Still, there must have been at least four or five thousand dollars, easily enough for his purposes.

"All right," said Arthur. "Now, keep quiet and everything will be fine." He backed out of the store, snatching a candy bar on the way. He had always loved sweets, and some things just never change.

As soon as he cleared the exit, Arthur bolted for the car. He dove into the passenger seat, and Matthew sped off into the night.

"Yeah, baby!" Arthur screamed. "We did it, man!" He hadn't felt this exhilarated since his childhood, and while he knew that his present elation had no significance, he was high enough to pretend.

"Did the guy put up a fight?" Matthew asked.

"Not at all. I'm pretty sure the dude pissed himself." Arthur laughed wildly.

"Where did you get the chocolate bar?" questioned Matthew, who was considerably more sober than his associate.

"I took it." Arthur laughed. "Sometimes you have to just steal shit and run."

He looked at the money in his lap, marveling at how easily he had stolen it and how helpless the clerk had been. Suddenly he was overcome with guilt, remembering his innocence with vague regret, experiencing a rare moment of lucidity.

But Arthur immediately dismissed such thoughts, electing to descend back into his comfortingly surreal world where morality was but one of many illogical demons. Life had taken everything from him— his father, his mother, his box—and it was about time he started taking back.

Chapter XXXI
Styx

Billy was distractedly downing his third beer when the doorbell rang. He sprung to his feet in surprise: he never had visitors, especially in the middle of the night. Hustling to the door, Billy opened it to find a teenage girl standing with her arms wrapped around her chest in the frigid darkness.

"Hi," she said kindly. "I'm so, so sorry to bother you this late, but I just really need to talk to Christopher. Is he here?"

"Chris?" Billy called loudly, genuinely unsure whether the boy was home.

"Yeah?"

"There's a girl who wants to talk to you." He turned toward her again. "What did you say your name was?"

Chris darted to the door. "Emily," he said, before she could reply. "How are you?"

"How are *you*?" she countered. "I haven't seen you in weeks."

"Would you like something to drink?" interrupted Billy. "Soda, coffee, beer? I've got lots of beer."

"Nothing for me, thanks," she said. "Can I come in? It's kind of freezing outside."

"Of course, of course," said Billy. "Sorry. I'm a bit drunk." He laughed and went to watch TV.

"So that's my uncle," Chris said amusedly, walking into the kitchen.

Emily grabbed his arm and pulled him close. "Christopher—"

"Chris," he corrected.

"Really? You never let me call you that."

"Well, that's my name now," he asserted, before picking out a beer bottle from the refrigerator.

"Anyway, Chris, we're really worried about you. I'm really worried about you."

"I'm fine," he said.

"I mean, you haven't shown up at school since...since it happened—which is perfectly understandable. But you haven't talked to me, or talked to anyone. And honestly, all those things you said at the funeral, they scared me. A lot."

"I'm fine," Chris repeated, taking a sip of beer.

"Are you?" Emily asked doubtfully. "Is it just that you didn't want to see me?"

"I always want to see you. I just don't want to go to school—maybe ever again. School, religion, government: it's all just shit."

"But you're a genius, Chris! You're the smartest person I've ever met. You owe it to yourself—no, to the world—to follow through on your education."

"I don't owe anyone anything," said Chris emphatically.

"Don't you want to be something? Don't you want to change things? I agree that sometimes life is shit, but you have the power to make it better. You saved me, Chris. You can save all of us."

"What does it matter, though? Everything is the way it is, and if I work hard and spend my life trying to make a difference, then some things might change. But really, what's the point? We're all just gonna die anyhow." He finished the bottle in his hand and turned away.

Emily hugged him from behind and whispered in his ear. "Come back, Chris. Come back. Everything is beautiful. I love you. God loves you."

Chris suddenly remembered Emily kissing Arthur, watched as she embraced the stranger himself. "You're just like the rest of them," he said quietly. "You're just like the rest of them."

"What?"

"I thought you were different," said Chris. "But you're not. Sure, you're pretty and smart. But as bright as you are, you're still just as deluded as everybody else. Can't you see that none of this shit is real? Why are you trying to convince me that it is?"

Emily started tearing up. "No, no. Chris, I'm not trying to—"

"Can you leave? Please?"

Emily was crying now. "I don't...I don't..."

"Goodbye, Emily."

She wiped her eyes and ran off. Stopping at the door, she turned around. "You had everything, Chris—the brain, the body, the heart—and you threw it away."

She shook her head. "So many times I've trusted people, only to be left alone in the dark. You were supposed to be different; you were supposed to show me the light again. But really, in spite of all your gifts, inside your soul is just as black as all the others. It's just as black as Arthur's." Then she was gone—the jilted lover, the companion star—ejected into the abyss. That was the last time she ever talked to Chris Wilson.

Billy walked into the room. "Women," he muttered, shaking his head.

* * *

Arthur had returned to his usual place at the rear of a ghastly parking lot, where he now stood under the veil of stinging drizzle and Stygian darkness. He hadn't been here since the shooting, afraid of a lethal encounter with Mr. Gates or one of his employees. But on this occasion, he had actually called Frankie, directing him to meet at midnight and bring his boss along. Suddenly, he heard footsteps splashing on the wet asphalt.

"Hey, Arthur!"

Arthur turned around. "Frankie, how's it going?"

"Put your hands up," Frankie ordered, making no pretense of friendship. "I have to search you before I can take you to Mr. Gates."

After thoroughly frisking Arthur for weapons, Frankie ushered him to an overflowing drainage ditch behind the parking lot. He ferried Arthur across the newly formed river, told him to stay where he was, and then retreated back from whence he came.

"Awfully brave, showing up here," said Mr. Gates, materializing on the other side of the water. He was shadowed by three henchmen this time, though he himself looked quite in control of this gloomy hell and clearly didn't need their protection.

"I got your money," Arthur announced flatly, holding up a wad of cash. "Six hundred dollars, just like you asked for, plus an extra four hundred for your patience."

"Confident little guy, aren't you?" Mr. Gates stared unswervingly at Arthur, whose face was largely hidden under his black hood. "So what, you show up here with a thousand bucks, give it to me, and then leave?"

"No," said Arthur. "I have an offer for you."

"Yeah? And what's that?"

Arthur paused. "I want to work for you," he said eventually.

Mr. Gates laughed. "Kid, you know I came here to kill you, right?"

"I know. Go ahead, if you want. I don't care. But believe me: it'll be much better for you if I'm on your side instead of this ditch."

"You sold my man fake dope and then disappeared, Arthur. Why would I ever hire you?"

"Because I'm smart; because I know the business. I got a partner, I got a gun, I got connections, and I got nothing to lose."

"All right, kid. For the sake of argument, let's say I take you up on this proposition. What would you be willing to do for me?"

"Anything," said Arthur, without hesitation. "Anything at all."

Mr. Gates—flanked by Frankie and his bodyguards—thought for several minutes, while meanwhile Arthur gazed across the river Styx at Hades, Charon, and Cerberus, the three-headed dog.

"Okay, you're in," Mr. Gates said finally. "You work for me now, Arthur."

"I'm not Arthur anymore," he brazenly declared, at that instant deciding he was sick of his name.

"Fine, then," said Mr. Gates. "What should I call you?"

"Black," he replied. "Call me Black."

Chapter XXXII
Waste

Chris had gone through somewhat of a falling-out with his emotions. Love had been noticeably absent from his life for half a decade—five long, monotonous years since Emily had knocked on his uncle's door. Wonder—among the first to go—had last shown its youthful face before his mother's passing. Even reliable Pain, tired of being ignored and resented, eventually left his mind barren, a wasteland. Surprisingly, Chris yearned for Pain most of all.

However, to say that he was entirely emotionless would be a slight overstatement, for perhaps his oldest companion still remained, hiding in the depths of his mind, repressed yet unmistakably present. Hatred—simmering, steaming, slithering like a slimy snake—punctuated his muted melancholy and gave him infrequent reminders that he was still alive. He hated society for brainwashing him. He hated the world for robbing him of his parents. And overwhelmingly, he hated Arthur.

In general, though, Chris felt nothing. He had cleansed himself of all addictions, but along with them had gone his precious antidote, which for so long had masked the world's brutal insignificance. Cured of desire, Chris was stricken with a far worse malady: the atrophy of his drive to the point of virtual nonexistence. He had dropped out of high school, while still technically maintaining perfect grades. Now he was just another burnout, working at the landfill with the rest of the refuse unfit for civilization.

"Chris!" called Uncle Billy. "Can you check out that patch over there? I got orders to squash down this whole section."

"Yeah, man," said Chris. He walked to where Billy was pointing, standing atop a literal mountain of garbage. The job actually proved less disagreeable than Chris had assumed; even the sickening smell had subsided after a week. Indeed, despite his academic prowess, Chris doubted that he was better suited for a desk job. At least here, beyond the realm of crushing civility, he had the illusion of freedom.

Scanning the disparate waste, Chris spotted an empty bottle of vodka. He was suddenly transported back to New Year's Eve at Emily's party, taking his first sip of alcohol, drinking his first drop of adulthood. Chris felt profoundly removed from that night, not just in time but perspective as well.

Next to the bottle lay a tattered newspaper, where a headline about recent crime escalation was printed in boldface. Chris sighed. Somewhere out there crept Arthur, cast in shadows, indifferent to the torment he inflicted on others: the stranger. Chris had abided by the dying request of his father, having not implicated his cousin despite his undying urge to do so. Yet Arthur had acted carelessly—as intoxicated people are wont to do—and his fingerprints on an empty pistol cartridge had pinned him as the culprit. Nevertheless, Arthur had successfully reinvented himself to foil his capture, forcing Chris to accept that justice was nothing more than another hollow promise.

Chris was about to give Billy the all-clear signal when he noticed the doll, a little plastic baby with a tiny plastic smile. Buried in humanity's debris, the doll was aglow with blissful radiance. Chris entered into a nostalgic trance.

"Everything good?" asked Billy.

Chris regained awareness of his surroundings. "Go ahead," he called back. Billy pushed a heavy lever, causing an enormous metal stamp to fall from the sky and crush the innocent figurine. Watching this scene unfold, young Christopher would have been severely traumatized. But the contemporary Chris quickly forgot about the incident, realizing that the doll was merely a fabrication, a societal construct, entirely artificial. Besides, he had already seen plenty of impressionable children and unwanted ideas meet their untimely demise. Today was a day like any other at the landfill, and Chris expected to experience many more days like it, week after week, month after month, year after year.

But Chris was not like Billy: he was not content wasting his life away. In the absence of purpose, he needed an antidote, an escape. A series of thoughts raced through his restless mind, eventually melding into a nefarious plan. Chris's lips curled into a rare smile. He was going to be a drug dealer.

* * *

Chris saw Jason right as he was about to leave. The two were basketball teammates in high school and had rekindled their connection as coworkers.

"Hey, Jason," Chris called out.

Jason turned around. "Chris, what's up?"

"Nothing much. I was just wondering...you sell drugs, don't you?"

Jason was totally caught off guard, his mouth fully agape.

"No, it's okay," said Chris. "The only reason I'm bringing it up is that I want in."

"*You* want to deal?" asked Jason skeptically.

"Yes," Chris replied, devoid of doubt.

"All right, I guess I can introduce you to my boss."

"Really? That would be great, man. Thanks."

"When do you want to meet him?"

"Uh, tomorrow night?"

"Sure thing. I'll make it happen."

"Sweet. So what's this dude like?"

"My boss? Well, he's a mysterious guy. Shaved head, dark clothes, always wears a hood. He's usually high, but even still he's really sharp. A genius, actually. Could've been a scientist if he wanted."

"Sounds like he knows what he's doing."

"Yeah, he's kind of an expert when it comes to the business. He's secretive too. No one knows where he's from. I don't even know his name."

"Then what do you call him?"

Jason looked Chris dead in the eye. "Black," he said. "Just Black."

Chris struggled to conceal his flaming reaction. "Don't tell him my name," he said, as nonchalantly as possible. "Just tell me where to find him."

* * *

The next night, Chris drifted into a godforsaken parking lot. Turning off his lights, he chose to remain in his car, waiting for his nemesis. After some time, an old-fashioned limousine rolled past him and stopped maybe twenty yards away. An imposing figure emerged from the passenger side, wielding a shotgun of commensurate bulk. He muttered something toward the limo, though what exactly he said was unclear, and then opened the backseat door for another man. Swathed in all black, this second figure was nearly invisible—a part of the darkness. But a momentary glance at his face revealed his identity: it was Arthur.

Chris shrunk down into his seat, attempting to stay hidden. Fortunately, his was not the only car in the lot, and neither man looked even once in his direction. Several minutes later, Arthur, growing impatient, got back into the limo and left. Chris slowly turned onto the street and followed his cousin, having suddenly discovered a reason to live, albeit a less than commendable one.

Chris tracked the limousine to the squalid outskirts of the city, making sure to keep his distance. They eventually arrived in front of a dilapidated home, where the large man escorted Arthur to the porch before departing. Chris watched from the safety of his car, memorized Arthur's address, and then drove off into the night. Rocketing through the wretched slum, he couldn't help grinning with unfamiliar satisfaction. Soon it would all be over. Soon he would have his revenge.

Chapter XXXIII
Black

Teardrop after teardrop rained down from the Seattle sky. The gibbous moon had long since surrendered its celestial domain, its audacity cloaked by gunmetal clouds. Rapids raced atop the once orderly streets, raging against the very bedrock of civilization, reasserting the rule of nature over man. The savage waters vaulted the curbs and trespassed onto the vacant sidewalks, in blatant defiance of the cedar sentries who guarded them. Somewhere a power line must have been damaged, for nothing permeated the primordial black. Nearly every creature lay asleep, not daring to venture out into the apocalypse.

Chris parked his car several blocks away from Arthur's house to ensure he would not be seen. Into the torrents he trudged, holding a small flashlight and his uncle's handgun, which he'd snatched the night before. He was clad in all black, including a jacket like the one his father had given him on the first day of school. A sea of crows suddenly swarmed down from the heavens, at ease with the darkness, and began squawking thunderously at Chris. Swimming through waves of rain and birds, he reached his destination.

From several days of reconnaissance, Chris had discovered that Arthur invariably kept his bedroom window open while he slept. But given the weather, it hardly seemed likely that the window was ajar, and sure enough Chris found it closed. He looked inside: Arthur wasn't there, which meant he must have been in another room, for he was certainly home. Not expecting the window to budge, he pulled up on its handle. Miraculously, it was unlocked—one sliver of carelessness the difference between life and death.

Chris snaked through the opening and tiptoed to the nightstand. From the drawer, he grasped Arthur's pistol, which he immediately recognized as the same one that had killed his father. Then and there, Chris resolved irrevocably to carry out his plan. He removed the ammunition and replaced the gun, then headed over to the bedroom door. Arthur could walk in at any moment, and when he did so, Chris would be ready.

* * *

Peering out from the two slits in his black mask, Chris looked into Arthur's eyes and saw his whole life: all his struggles and successes, his wishes and his fears. Most disturbingly, though, Chris saw himself. He shook—trembling beneath the weight of truth. Unable to stand his reflection any longer, Chris aimed his gun and fired. The bullet went through Arthur's eye and into his brain, killing him instantly. At that moment, Chris realized for the first time that he, not Arthur, was the stranger: he had lost his mother, he had stopped caring about society and its rules, and now he was a murderer.

Chris dragged Arthur's body through his filthy residence and out the door. He pushed his cousin onto the flooded ground, watching Black's blood mix with the black river under the black sky. Chris removed his black gloves and his black mask, revealing his defining scar. He threw his black jacket into the black house, and walked into the wet, black street. Nothing mattered now. It was over. It was finally over.

* * *

As Chris started into the storm, crows circled him with furious speed, not squawking as they had earlier. A few landed on his shoulders, but he continued on unfazed. No longer was he afraid of the crows, no longer did he fear their omen of death. The water below him swirled around his legs like a vortex, and the air whooshed past his chest with hurricane force. Chris had transformed into the ultimate bringer of destruction: a black hole.

Suddenly, he began to cry, something he had not done in ages. Teardrop after teardrop rained down from his withered core, the last remaining emotions of a now truly emotionless man. Left without purpose, without reason, without joy, Chris pressed the gun against his head. He had no delusions of grandeur; there was nothing romantic about his conclusion. He had lived, and now, meaninglessly, he would die.

Chris squeezed the trigger. The bullet shattered his skull, finally setting him free from his intellectual prison. Ironically, yet somehow fittingly, he'd met the same fate as his greatest foe—his death also forgotten in a universe where life is the exception. His uncle's gun, an anachronism in this ancient tale, sank down to the street, swallowed up by the suburban swells. Black blood seeped from Chris's reopened scar as the tides took hold of his body and carried him into oblivion.

At that instant, a new star was born. Perhaps it will uncover the meaning of everything, perhaps not. The story of Christopher Wilson, however, is that of a star that never really was, a glimmer of brilliant light extinguished by a cold, unfeeling universe. Society had tried its best to keep him in blinding white, but he had seen through the ruse. Maybe one day the new star will enlighten the world, but for now its glow was infinitely distant, and absolute darkness reigned supreme.